Rock Star
SUPERSTAR

ALSO BY BLAKE NELSON

The New Rules of High School

Girl

Exile

User

Rock Star SUPERSTAR

BLAKE NELSON

Viking

VIKING

Published by Penguin Group

Penguin Young Readers Group, 345 Hudson Street, New York, New York 10014, U.S.A.

Penguin Group (Canada), 10 Alcorn Avenue, Toronto, Ontario, Canada M4V 3B2
(a division of Pearson Penguin Canada Inc.)

Penguin Books Ltd, 80 Strand, London WC2R 0RL, England

Penguin Ireland, 25 St Stephen's Green, Dublin 2, Ireland
(a division of Penguin Books Ltd)

Penguin Group (Australia), 250 Camberwell Road, Camberwell, Victoria 3124,
Australia (a division of Pearson Australia Group Pty Ltd)

Penguin Books India Pvt Ltd, 11 Community Centre, Panchsheel Park,
New Delhi - 110 017, India

Penguin Group (NZ), Cnr Airborne and Rosedale Roads, Albany, Auckland,
New Zealand (a division of Pearson New Zealand Ltd)

Penguin Books (South Africa) (Pty) Ltd, 24 Sturdee Avenue, Rosebank, Johannesburg
2196, South Africa

Penguin Books Ltd, Registered Offices: 80 Strand, London WC2R 0RL, England

First published in 2004 by Viking, a division of Penguin Young Readers Group

1 3 5 7 9 10 8 6 4 2

LIBRARY OF CONGRESS CATALOGING-IN-PUBLICATION DATA

Nelson, Blake, date.

Rock star, superstar / by Blake Nelson.

p. cm.

Summary: When Pete, a talented bass player, moves from playing in the high school
jazz band to playing in a popular rock group, he finds the experience exhilarating even
as his new fame jeopardizes his relationship with girlfriend Margaret.

ISBN 0-670-05933-1 (hardcover)

[1. Bands (Music)—Fiction. 2. Musicians—Fiction. 3. Rock music—Fiction.] I. Title.

PZ7.B4328Ro 2004

[Fic]—dc22

2003027556

Printed in U.S.A.   Set in Meridien   Book design by Nancy Brennan

★ ★ ★

for my dad

BIG THANKS: Regina Hayes and Catherine Frank, Charlotte Sheedy and Carolyn Kim, Sharyn November, Nancy Brennan, Hadley Hooper. Jennifer Hubert Swan, Laural and Joanna—and all librarians everywhere. Underground publishers: Don Waters and John De Witt at VERSUS PRESS. NYC: Beth Rosenberg, Nick, Maszle, Skeegs, Gordon, Frieda and Nora, Ben Schrank, Casey Kait, Janet Capron, Jackie Phelan. Portland: Sally, Ana, Johnny Morrow, everyone at Powells, Craig Lesley, Jonathan Nicholas, Marne, the Sherriest, Drew and Heidi, Penny and the boys, my mum. Music people: Carl Boland, Bryon Lyons, Rich D'Albiss, Robin Cornell, Courtney and Kat, Jem Cohen, John Shonle, Jeff Williams (the Ziplocs), Otis P. Otis (the Posers), Henry Rollins (who found "The Tiny Masters" in the dense thicket of Nietszche). And especially John Fahs.

In the days when you were hopelessly poor
I just liked you more

—*The Smiths*

Contents

★ ★ ★

Mad Skillz

It was April and raining lightly as I drove my dad's car to band practice. I didn't usually get the car, so I took my time, tuning the radio, adjusting the windshield wipers, feeling the power of being on my own. At a red light I played drums on the steering wheel and casually looked at the drivers in the other cars, hoping for a girl, or someone from my school to see me driving. But it was all grown-ups: moms with kids, dads, office people going home from work.

The light turned green, and I drove. The rain fell. On the radio, Hits 101 wasn't playing anything good, so I tried some other stations. There was nothing. Commercials. Talk radio. Then I found Queens of the Stone Age on the New Rock station. The song was "Go with the Flow," which if you listened closely had a piano in it. I loved stuff like that, a piano in a hard rock song. A casual listener wouldn't even notice, but there it was, banging along in the background, giving the whole song a certain brightness and bounce. That was the kind of thing an average musician wouldn't think of. That's what separated the men from the boys.

At Dosche Road I swung a left and took the long way up the hill. That was a better drive—the road was curvy and narrow, you could lean into the curves, you could push it a little. At the top of the hill, I turned left so I could cruise by Rotter's grocery store. I had seen Sarah Vandeway there a couple of weeks ago, standing outside with her cell phone. Not that I would know what to do if she were standing there now. Pull in? Pretend to buy something? *Hey Sarah, what's up?* No, I would probably just keep driving.

But it was something to think about. I was sixteen. At some point I would have to deal with girls. I couldn't imagine having a girlfriend, but a year ago I couldn't have imagined being in a band. And I was in one. Mad Skillz, we were called. And I was only a sophomore. So anything was possible. Or at least, things that appeared faraway did happen eventually. Bands, girls, graduation. High school seemed pretty endless, but it was only four years.

★ ★ ★ 2 ★ ★ ★

Mad Skillz practiced at Eric Simon's house. I parked across the street and pulled my bass out of the backseat. I was halfway up the driveway when Eric came out of the garage. "Bro!" he said. "Guess what? We got the gig!"

Eric had been trying to get Mad Skillz hired to play the Spring Dance at Evergreen High, where we all went to school. No student band had ever played it before.

"No way," I said.

"For real! We got it! The student council guy said we sounded way better than the other bands," said Eric. "And they like our song selection."

"The classic rock," I said.

"The classic rock. That's it. That's what they wanted."

Todd Harrison pulled up in his pickup truck. He was our lead guitarist. "Todd!" said Eric. "Guess what?"

Todd Harrison was the rock star of our band. He was also a senior, so he never got too worked up about anything.

"We got the Spring Dance!" said Eric.

Even ultracool Todd Harrison was impressed. "No kidding?" he said, lifting his guitar case out of his truck.

"We'll be playing to our own school," said Eric. "And we're getting eight hundred bucks!"

"Eight hundred bucks," said Todd. "I like the sound of that." He high-fived Eric. Eric high-fived me. All three of us tried to high-five, but it didn't really work.

The fourth person in Mad Skillz was Daniel Fincher, our drummer. He was late, as usual, but when he heard the news, he nodded his approval. "Finally," he said. "People will know I'm in a band."

We went downstairs to Eric's basement and began to tune up. Eric gestured for quiet. "You know, since we got the big gig," he said, "I've been thinking."

Todd groaned.

"No seriously," continued Eric. "I think we should do something about our look."

"What about it?" said Daniel. He was sitting behind his drums, adjusting his cymbals.

"We need to look more professional."

"Like what?" said Daniel again. I said nothing, it was me he was probably talking about. They had complained about my "look" before.

"You know," said Eric. "Like add a little flair to the visual part of the band."

I was wearing my usual clothes: a shirt from the Gap, baggy khakis, Reebok shoes.

"You know," said Eric. "We're supposed to be cool musicians. We shouldn't look like every other high school student."

"You mean me," I said.

"You . . ." said Eric. "And maybe Daniel a little bit, and me too, I'm just as bad." Eric was very diplomatic.

"I thought we were about the music," I said. "Not dressing up."

"How do you know if you've never tried it?" said Eric.

"What do you want us to wear?" said Daniel.

"Just something . . ." said Eric, thinking about it. "Well, like we could all get red Converse high-tops. Something like that maybe."

"Red high-tops?" said Daniel. "That's so eighties."

"Yeah but the eighties are back, right?"

"I don't want to wear something everyone else is wearing," said Todd who, as I mentioned, was the rock star of our group. He had hair that he gelled meticulously, and sideburns, and old jeans with carefully groomed holes in the knees.

"We could get suits," said Daniel.

"Suits are cool," said Eric. "The problem is how do you

clean them? And they get hot in the stage lights. And what if we can't find matching ones?"

"I'm not wearing matching *anything*," said Todd. "Especially in front of my own school."

"Well what do *you* think we should do?" Eric asked him.

Todd looked around at the three of us. He looked at me. "You're the worst," he said, with the disdain that seniors can use on sophomores. "Don't you have some cool jeans or something?"

I shrugged.

"I think red Converse high-tops would solve the problems," said Eric. "They're cheap, they're cool. And we can pay for them out of the band fund."

Todd was skeptical.

"And it'll give us a clean-cut thing," continued Eric. "And maybe we can do more high school dances, instead of junior high stuff and parties."

"Why do we have to dress up?" I said. "Why can't the music stand by itself?"

"Dude," said Daniel, from behind his drums. "We play covers. It's not even our music."

"Of course the music stands by itself," Eric said. "We're Mad Skillz. It's always about the music for us. But that's the industry. You have to compromise. You have to incorporate some showmanship."

"Okay, okay," said Todd. "That's enough about *the industry*. Can we get on with practice now?"

"Will you at least think about it?" said Eric.

We all agreed we would.

7

★★★ 3 ★★★

That night I couldn't sleep. I kept thinking about the Spring Dance. We were going to play live, onstage, in front of our entire school. Finally I got up and went into the basement of our house. My dad and I had a little studio down there, with amps and guitars and keyboards. It was soundproofed so the neighbors wouldn't complain. I plugged in my bass and started messing around.

A half hour later the door opened. It was my dad. He couldn't sleep either. He was in his bathrobe, a drink in hand. He grinned, and I grinned back. It was a joke we had: we were the "Sleepless McGradys."

He shut the door all the way so we wouldn't wake the neighbors. He turned on his guitar and sat and played some jazz chords. I started "So What?" which is a Miles Davis jam we often played—especially when we couldn't sleep and it was late at night. "So What?" does a back and forth thing between the guitar and bass. My dad and I had played it a million times. It was like warm milk for musicians.

After that I told him about the Spring Dance. I explained they didn't usually let student bands play it, but we sounded so pro they were giving us a shot. My dad was impressed.

"Eric wants us to wear these dumb shoes though," I said. "He wants us to get matching Converse high-tops."

"Yeah?" said my dad.

"It's sort of dumb, don't you think?"

My dad smiled. "It could be worse. I wore some stupid stuff in my day."

"Really?" I said. "Like what?"

"Oh God, one band I was in, they wanted us all in spandex pants."

"Really? You had spandex pants?"

"Actually, I borrowed them, which is even worse."

"You *borrowed* spandex pants?"

He laughed. "Matching shoes aren't that bad," he said, going back to his guitar. He played a little blues riff. It was Hendrix, who was my dad's all-time favorite.

I fell in, and we jammed it out.

Everyone in my family is a musician. My dad was big in the Seattle scene in the eighties. So was my mom, who did more acoustic singer-songwriter stuff. My dad always said my mom would have been the most famous of everyone, but she died of cancer before she could record her first album.

My dad was more of a hard rock guy. One of his last bands had the same A&R guy as Guns N' Roses. That band broke up though, and then my mom died, and after that my dad focused more on studio stuff and giving private lessons. He never joined another real band. Now he taught music at Portland State. He still played out now and then, sitting in with friends. He could play anything: jazz, country, rock, blues. He was pretty amazing.

It was three o'clock in the morning when we went back upstairs. I crawled back to bed. I felt like I could sleep now. It always helped talking over music stuff with my dad. Like whatever goofy plan Eric or those guys came up with, my dad had seen it before. And the cool thing was, he never looked down on Mad Skillz. Even though we were a cover band, even though we played a Britney Spears song, he always encouraged me. I mean, sometimes I got the feeling he would rather I didn't become a professional musician. You know, like maybe I could get a normal job. But how do you do that? I wasn't good at school. I was good at the bass.

The next day Eric stopped by my locker at school. It was official: we were all getting red Converse high-tops. The problem was I had jazz band that week too. Mr. Moran, the Evergreen jazz band teacher, was already mad at me for missing two rehearsals. We had the state competition in Pendleton in June, which was only six weeks away. We weren't very good, and he was counting on me to anchor the rhythm section, so I had to be at rehearsals.

Also, where did you get red Converse high-tops? I had no idea. I knew Eric would send me downtown, and if I said I didn't have time he would complain about my lack of commitment and why was I even in jazz band anyway? Didn't I know how geeky it was? So I looked around soph/frosh wing to see if anyone wore stuff like that. No one did. Why would they? Who wants to look ridiculous?

Then Margaret Little walked by my locker. She was wearing red Converse high-tops, the exact ones I needed. She was one of the freaks of our class, but whatever, I stopped her and asked where she got them. She said Woodridge Mall. She tried to tell me which store, but I never went to the mall, so I didn't know. She offered to draw me a map.

After school that day I went to jazz band, but Mr. Moran was sick, so rehearsal was cancelled. This was my chance to go to the mall. I went to the bus stop, and who was there but Margaret Little. She was wearing a black overcoat, her red high-tops, a weird vintage dress. It was her "punk librarian" look.

I hesitated when I saw her. Margaret Little was not someone you wanted to be seen hanging out with. Freshman year she had written a poem called "Thoughts" that got published in the school paper. Everyone made fun of her about it. It became a school joke. Also her best friend was a skinny girl named Lauren Melucci, who everyone said was anorexic.

It started to rain, so I had no choice but to stand inside the bus stop. When Margaret saw me she asked if I was going to get my shoes. I nodded I was. She said she was going to the mall too, to get some stationery for her mom's birthday.

"That's nice," I said.

"You don't go to the mall very much?" she said.

"No, I don't have time."

"The mall downtown has better stuff . . . but Woodridge is okay."

"Yeah," I said, staring at the wet road. I didn't want to get into a long conversation.

"Do you want me to show you the store where they have the shoes?"

"That's all right," I said. "I can probably find it."

"I don't mind. I can take you right there."

I had looked at her map, and it was pretty confusing. So I said all right.

Unfortunately, that meant sitting with her on the bus. I wasn't too thrilled about that. She took the window seat, and I considered sitting in the seat behind her like I would with a guy friend—so we could sit long ways with our feet on the seat. There were other people on the bus though, so I had to sit beside her. I kept as far away as I could.

She started talking as soon as the bus moved. She said her mom was having a poem published in *Oregon Magazine of Arts and Crafts*. Her mom had been working on it for three months, this one little poem. So for her birthday Margaret was getting her special paper and her older sister was getting her a special pen so she could write more poems and hopefully get them published too.

"That's nice," I said.

"Why are you getting red high-tops?" she asked.

"I'm in a band. We all have to get them."

"You're in a band?" she said. "Really? What kind of band is it?"

"We play dances and stuff. We play Top Forty, classic rock."

"Oh," she said. "That makes more sense I guess. You don't really seem like a high-tops kind of guy."

"Yeah, I'm not into looking weird," I said. "I mean, no offense to you or whatever."

She stared at me. "Why do you say that?" she asked. "Do you think I look weird?"

"You dress like an old lady," I said. "And you wear all black."

"But my shoes are red," she said.

"Yeah, but that just makes it weirder."

"Do you think weird is bad?"

"I don't know," I said. I looked out the window. "I just don't want to get beat up. Or have people think I'm a freak."

She stared at me.

"Not that you're a freak," I said.

"I just dress like one?"

"Well . . . yeah," I said. "No offense."

"No offense taken," she said.

We sat in silence after that. It sort of bummed me out. I hadn't meant to be so harsh. I was just trying to be honest.

★ ★ ★ **5** ★ ★ ★

She must not have been too offended, because at the mall, Margaret started talking again. She knew a lot about Woodridge Mall. She told me about the different stores, the different shops, the different people who hung out at them. Eventually she led me to a place called Girl Talk.

"I'm not going in there," I said.

"Why not?"

"It's a store for girls. I'm not a girl, in case you haven't noticed."

"It's not *only* for girls. They have red high-tops. Nobody else has them."

As we stood there, two girls went inside with their boyfriends.

"See?" she said. "Nobody's going to think anything."

I went in. It was still embarrassing. The saleswoman came over, and Margaret said, "He needs red Converse high-tops." I was obviously embarrassed, but the woman said not to worry, a lot of boys bought shoes there. Margaret made me sit down. I took off my Reeboks and my feet smelled. Margaret grimaced and waved her hand in her face. I apologized to the saleswoman when she returned. She said it was okay. She gave me the red high-tops and I put them on. They were pretty flimsy shoes. They felt strange on my feet, not like my Reeboks, which had a reinforced arch support and interior foam cushioning and high-test, shock-resistant soles. The high-tops didn't have anything. They were soft though, and comfortable. Margaret stood over me. The saleslady did too. They both wanted to know if I liked them. I shrugged. The truth was, I didn't like them. They were *bright red*. I sure as hell wasn't going to wear them anywhere except onstage. But the band was paying for them, so whatever. I put my old shoes back on and went to the cashier.

I thought that would be the end of Margaret, but after Girl Talk she stayed with me. She talked more about the stationery she was getting her mom and about poetry and how hard it is to write. I couldn't believe she kept talking about poetry. Her poem "Thoughts" had made her the laughingstock of our whole school.

When we came to the stationery store, she asked if I

would come in. I couldn't think of a good excuse, so I said okay. She was talking a lot now, and she seemed nervous. She also kept looking at me. I suddenly thought *What if she likes me?* Was that possible? We barely knew each other. And we couldn't be more different. And anyway, I wasn't exactly popular. No girls had ever liked me before.

I watched Margaret flip through the stationery, and suddenly I was nervous too. Fortunately, she was still talking. She had the stationery choice narrowed down to two different kinds, which one did I think was best? I picked one at random. She thought that was a good choice, and we went to the register.

While she paid I stood behind her. I watched her hands and her shoulders and the back of her head. *Could I like someone like her?* She was kind of chubby, which was the other thing people made fun of her about. And she talked so much. And of course she dressed like a freak. But her face was okay. She had pretty eyes. And she was nice at least. . . .

I stopped myself. What was I thinking? This was *Margaret Little*, author of "Thoughts." There was no way.

$$\star\,\star\,\star\;\mathbf{6}\;\star\,\star\,\star$$

Two weeks later we played the Spring Dance. We all wore our red Converse high-tops. No one seemed to notice though. Nobody even looked at the stage.

We opened with "Back in Black," the AC/DC classic, which people always like. It didn't have much effect though;

not many people were there yet. Also the acoustics in the gym were terrible. You could barely tell which song we were playing.

About four songs in, my dad stopped by. He had never seen us, so that was cool. He stood to the side and nodded his head to the beat. Unfortunately he was still there when we did our Britney Spears song. Eric sang it in a falsetto that never sounded right. My dad understood. He kind of winked at me during the worst of it. Then he waved and took off. From the way he was dressed, he probably had a date.

After the first set we hung out behind the stage. The turnout was less than we expected, so Eric was a little upset. He cheered up when two girls came behind the stage. He went into rock star mode: shaking their hands and asking them how they were enjoying the show. They looked a little confused. They were looking for the bathroom.

By the second set it was clear that the dance was not going to fill up. Eric took this personally, though I knew it had nothing to do with us. People don't go to high school dances based on what band is playing.

Afterward, while we packed up the equipment, the student council guy tried to cheer us up. We would still get paid, he promised. Eric was pissed though. There had been no applause after our last song, so we couldn't do our encore. No one had "put their hands in the air" during our Outkast medley. No one had noticed that we were students and not a bunch of middle-aged hacks. Didn't people know how cool that was? We actually *went* to Evergreen.

Todd was pissed too. He didn't have a girlfriend, and he always expected some girl to throw herself at him at one of our gigs.

That was the difference between those guys and me. I knew the reality of being a musician. Like my dad always said about famous bands who seem to party all the time: the reality was, famous bands work their asses off. They played up the partying for the media. It was part of the image. Like David Lee Roth and the whiskey bottle he used to drink from onstage. It was full of iced tea.

And I knew it anyway from being in jazz band. Girls aren't going to love you because you can play an instrument. All that stuff about free sex and wild parties, that was a myth. The people who believed that stuff the most were the bands who never made it. It was the Todd Harrisons of the world, the wannabes, who kept the myth going.

★★★ 7 ★★★

At school my main nonmusic friend was Robert Hatch, who lived down the street from me. He was a computer genius and kind of a geek. That was okay, since I was in jazz band, which technically made me a geek too.

One day at lunch I was sitting with Robert and some of his computer buddies when Margaret Little and Lauren came to our table. Margaret asked me how the Spring Dance went. I said it went okay. She nodded. She asked how the shoes were. I said they were okay. She nodded some more.

17

"I heard your band was good," she said.

"We were okay," I said. "You should have come."

"I don't really like Top Forty music."

I was trying to be polite until she said that. Now I turned to her. "We don't just play Top Forty," I said. "We happen to play some pretty serious stuff, some pretty complicated stuff."

"I know," she said. "Oh and by the way, my mother really liked the paper you picked out."

"I didn't pick it," I said.

"You helped," she said. Then she sat down. Right next to me. Right in front of everyone.

"I didn't pick out the paper," I repeated, scooting away. "You did."

She ignored this. "Have you seen *Live in My Bedroom*?"

Live in My Bedroom was a new movie about a high school kid who has to join his favorite band when their singer gets kidnapped in his city. I did want to see it. But not with her.

"Have you?" she asked again.

"No," I said. Margaret was staring at me now. Lauren was staring at me too.

"Do you want to go see it this weekend?" said Margaret.

I felt my face start to burn. "With you?" I said.

"Yeah."

I didn't want to. I didn't want to at all. I glanced at Robert. I looked farther down the table. Every guy at that table was staring at me like W*ow, a girl is asking Pete out!* Robert's mouth was actually hanging open. I didn't see how I could say no.

So I said okay.

+++

Later that day, I regretted it. I had never gone to a movie with a girl before. I had never done *anything* with a girl before. To have my first time be with Margaret Little, someone I didn't even *like*. . . .

I talked to Robert Hatch as we walked down the hall.

"But she's perfect for you," he said.

"Are you crazy? In what way is she perfect for me?"

"She's all punk and stuff. And you're in a band."

"I'm not in a *punk* band."

"What difference does it make. Bands are cool. She's cool."

"She's not cool. She's a freak. She wrote 'Thoughts.'"

"What's that?"

"That poem last year? Everyone made fun of her?"

"Whatever. So she writes poetry. What do you expect? Those are the girls that go for musicians."

I shook my head. "I don't care. I'm not doing it."

"What girl would you go out with?" he asked.

"A normal girl. A pretty girl. Someone like Sarah Vandeway."

"Sarah Vandeway?" Robert laughed. "Sarah Vandeway wouldn't go out with you in a million years. Those girls like seniors and popular guys. You're a musician. Girls like Margaret Little is what musicians get."

"I don't care. I'm still not doing it."

"You kind of have to now," he said, veering off toward his locker. "You already said you would."

★★★ **8** ★★★

On Friday, after school, I had jazz band. It was May and warm, and going to the rehearsal room, I had to walk through people playing Frisbee and lounging on the lawn. It was hard to focus on jazz band at the end of the year. All we had left was the state competition, where we were going to get slaughtered anyway. Last year, we were pretty good and we didn't even make the top ten. This year we'd lost a bunch of our best people. We would be lucky to not come in last.

The rehearsal began. I stood with my bass next to Kevin, the drummer. Kevin was the clown of jazz band. He spent most rehearsals throwing Skittles at people or trying to look down the front of Pam Olson's shirt during her saxophone solos.

After rehearsal Kevin and I sometimes hung out and jammed. Today he hurried off. He had just joined a rock band of his own. He had been jealous of me for being in Mad Skillz and playing to "junior high chicks," so he was psyched to have his own band finally. They didn't have a name yet. It was two brothers, Nick and Billy Carlisle. They had gone to Bradley Day School, though they had graduated a couple years before. They weren't very good musicians, according to Kevin, so they weren't doing dances. They were more of a jam band from the sounds of it—not that there's anything wrong with that.

+++

I got home early and did a little homework. I was having a pretty good sophomore year. I had a possible A in Spanish and at least a B in math, which was pretty good for me. I was getting a C+ in English though, and my world cultures teacher, Mr. Gruder, hated me and I would be lucky to get a C. After I got most of my Spanish done I made a frozen pizza and turned on the TV.

My dad must have stayed in the city after his class, because he got home late. His eyes looked like he'd been partying. He probably had a date. He had a girlfriend all through my freshman year, but they broke up, so now he was dating again. That got a little weird sometimes, though he generally kept his romantic life separate from me.

"Hey," I said from the couch. "I made a frozen pizza. There's some still in the oven."

He nodded. He made himself a drink. He didn't go anywhere near the oven.

He came into the living room and sat on the couch. "How you doing?" he said.

"Fine," I said, staring at the TV.

"Wuddya do in school today?" he asked. That question never sounded right coming out of his mouth.

"Nothing. Jazz band."

My dad drank half his drink in one slug. He had definitely been on a date. I could smell something feminine on him, perfume, something an older woman would wear—that and the smell of the alcohol. He was really drunk.

"Actually. I think I'm going to crash," I said. "I got a Spanish test tomorrow."

"All right," said my dad.

I stood up and put my plate in the sink. I noticed the oven was still on. I turned it off and put the last of the pizza in the fridge.

$$\star\star\star\ 9\ \star\star\star$$

My date with Margaret was on Friday night. Robert came over. He was amazed I wasn't wearing my best clothes or putting on deodorant. I was just going. "It wasn't even my idea," I reminded him. He said that didn't matter, it was still a date. She was still a girl.

Margaret had given me her address and tried to draw a map, but it wasn't much help. I found it anyway. I parked the car in front of the house and went to the door. I rang the doorbell. It played a little song: *ding dang dung dong.* Her front yard had a little rock garden in it.

The door opened. It was her mom. "You must be Peter," she said, "Come in, come in." I did. The house smelled strange. It had carpeting everywhere—it was spongy to walk on. Her mom was watching a knitting show on TV. She turned it off and asked if I wanted something to drink.

"No thanks," I said.

"Margaret tells me you're in the jazz band at school," said Mrs. Little.

"Yeah," I said. "I play bass."

Her mom thought that was great. The inside of their

house was nice in that suburban way. There were paintings on the walls, and bookshelves.

I heard a door close and Margaret came around the corner. She had eye makeup on and a white hair band on her head. Everything else she wore was black. Except for her red Converse high-tops. It was weird but it was okay. I was glad she had dressed up. I didn't know why exactly.

We left and walked to my car. I opened her door for her because Robert said I had to. I got in my side. I had thought up this little speech, about how this wasn't a date, it was just going to the movies, we were just friends and I didn't want there to be any misunderstandings. I didn't say it though. I was afraid to. Maybe my wrinkly, untucked shirt said it for me.

The movie theater at the mall was crowded. A lot of people were there on dates. I hadn't thought about that. It was a little embarrassing.

When we got to the front of the ticket line *Live in My Bedroom* was sold out. I didn't know what to do, but Margaret quickly suggested the horror movie that was playing in twenty minutes. We got tickets to that. We had to wait though.

We went to the food court. We got Cokes and sat and watched people. She asked me about Spanish, since we had been in Spanish class together freshman year. I said I was doing okay. She said she was getting an A in Spanish. She was also getting an A in English, world cultures and personal economics. She was worried she might get a B in biology. She said her hardest class was PE, because she was uncoordinated and she needed to lose ten pounds and everyone always told her that. I told her she looked okay, she didn't look fat or anything.

A guy from my English class walked by. He saw me and said, "Hey, Pete, I saw your band at the dance!"

"Thanks," I said.

"I should have gone to see you guys," said Margaret. "Sorry."

"It doesn't matter," I said.

The movie was pretty good. The plot didn't make sense, but there was a lot of blood and a girl in her underwear got chopped up. I was worried Margaret might grab me or hold my arm during one of the scary parts. She didn't. She even moved her arm away when I put mine on the armrest. Later though, when her arm was on it, I put mine next to hers to see what she would do. She left hers where it was. Not that it made a difference. I mean, so our arms were touching, so what? It didn't mean anything.

★ ★ ★ 10 ★ ★ ★

The mall was closed when the movie let out, so you couldn't walk around. I said I had to go home anyway, so we rode down the escalator to the parking lot. Other people from the movie rode down with us. They were talking and laughing. Margaret and I barely said a word.

In the parking lot a bunch of kids stood around a car, listening to a new rap record. I couldn't tell which rapper it was, but it had a cool guitar riff. I stopped walking for a second to listen. Margaret waited. She was being really quiet. I think she was upset I didn't want to do something after the movie. Or maybe she was sad, like maybe until that point she hadn't noticed I didn't like her. Now that I was eager to go home, she saw what the reality was. In the car she gave me directions, like where to turn to take her home. She wasn't talking at all. And since she usually talked, it was total silence.

I started to feel bad. I turned on the radio to cover up the awkwardness. There was nothing good on.

Finally, I broke down. "I guess I don't have to go straight home," I said. "If you want to do something else."

"That's okay," she said.

"It's only ten-fifteen. We could go to Denny's. I'm kind of hungry."

"Are you sure?"

We went to Denny's. We got a booth, and she ordered a salad and I ordered a waffle and we ate. She was still not talking, so I talked about the rap song we had heard at the mall. I talked about other rap stuff and how in rap, the stuff going on in the background was really amazing and really technically advanced. Of course rap guys didn't have actual bands like rock groups, it was mostly studio musicians, but studio guys were usually better than guys in bands anyway. Especially the old sessions guys who had been around forever. . . .

Margaret listened to everything I said—or at least she pretended to. She seemed happy though. I felt better too. Like finally I was relaxed and feeling comfortable. I ate some of her salad and she ate some of my waffle. We sort of smiled at each other.

+++

At her house I kissed her good night. I didn't plan to, it just happened. And then it kind of kept going. During it, I felt a vague panic, like if we kissed too much, would that mean something? But I thought of all the guy conversations I had heard about doing stuff with girls. You were basically supposed to try for whatever you could get, whenever you could get it.

When we stopped kissing, she looked into her lap. I looked out my window. When she turned to me she had this surprised look on her face. Like she couldn't believe what had happened. I couldn't believe it either. "I better go inside," she said.

"Yeah," I said. "I better go too."

★★★ 11 ★★★

I didn't talk to Margaret over the weekend. On Monday, I watched for her in the halls. I didn't know what I was going to say to her. I didn't know what was going to happen.

After second period, I was kneeling down at my locker, pulling on my biology textbook, which was buried under a bunch of other stuff. I saw Margaret coming down the hall. I swallowed. I focused on my textbook.

She came up behind me. "Hi, Peter," she said. She was nervous. I could hear it in her voice.

"Hi," I said, not looking up.

"What are you doing?"

"Trying to get this book out."

"Oh," she said. She watched me.

I got the book out but I stayed where I was, rearranging the other stuff at the bottom of the locker.

"I wanted to ask you something," she said.

"What?"

She lowered her voice to a whisper. "You know how we went to the movie?"

"Yeah?"

"Well . . ." She took a deep breath. "I was thinking, if you want, maybe we could do something else. Maybe you could walk me home after school?"

I stared at my book. "I have jazz band after school."

"Oh," she said.

I stood up. I didn't look at her. I dug through my locker shelf for a pen.

"Well, if you want, you could come over afterward," she continued. "My mom doesn't get home till six."

I tried to think about it. All I could think about was us making out in the car. The truth was, I liked it. The truth was, I wanted to do it again.

"Do you think . . ." she said. "You might want to?"

I was too afraid to look at her. I was too afraid to do anything. Somehow, out of my mouth, came the words: "Yeah, okay."

After jazz band I walked to her house. The skies were gray and overcast, and I looked up at them as I walked. I thought, *At this moment I am walking to a girl's house.*

When I got there I rang the doorbell. *Ding dang dung dong.*

The door opened.

"Hi," she said.

"Hey," I said.

She waved me inside and shut the door. We stood in the entrance way. She had changed into jeans and a T-shirt. She looked sort of hot.

"What do you want to do?" she asked.

"I don't know. It's your house."

"Wanna go in the basement?"

"Okay."

We went in the basement. We sat on a couch. She kept squirming around on her side. She had a huge grin on her face.

"What's so funny?" I said.

"Nothing," she said, grinning.

We made out. It was like in the car, but better. We had more room. We could do it for as long as we wanted.

After that she took me upstairs to her bedroom and we made out on her bed. She showed me pictures of her little sister and her parents at their beach house. We made out some more.

Later, we went to her kitchen. At six her mom would get home, so we had to be careful. We made microwave popcorn and talked about school. At 5:45 I left.

In her garage we kissed. She looked up into my face. She had the prettiest blue eyes. "Do you want to be boyfriend and girlfriend?" she asked.

"Do you?"

She nodded.

"Okay," I said.

"But only if you want to," she said.

"I want to."

"Okay," she said. She ran back into her house.

Jazz Band

★ ★ ★ 12 ★ ★ ★

The first weekend of June was the state jazz competition. It was held in Pendleton, Oregon, which was high desert country, about six hours to the east. It's where they make Pendleton shirts.

Kevin and I and the rest of the band waited in the back parking lot after school on Friday. Kevin was eating Skittles and occasionally throwing them at the hood of Pam Olson's sweatshirt, trying to get them to stay in.

Mr. Moran pulled up with the bus, and we all crowded in and began the long drive to Pendleton. Jazz band wasn't the greatest in terms of what kind of music you played, but the other stuff, like going to Pendleton for a weekend, made up for it.

I sat with Kevin and hoped he would calm down. He was a junior, but he was hyper. He wasn't even that good of a drummer. Our drummer in Mad Skillz, Daniel Fincher, was way better. Daniel was classically trained and had won a bronze medal in the Drumming Olympics.

After harassing our freshman trumpet player for a while, Kevin turned on his Discman and crashed. While he slept, I looked through his CDs. He had all these underground bands I'd never heard of. I looked at a couple of them. They had weird names, weird song titles. Death Cab for Cutie, Interpol, Hot Hot Heat. Why did some bands try so hard to be weird? Why couldn't they just be good?

After three hours we stopped at a truck stop to eat. I went into the little store and found a postcard with a cartoon of a drunk cowboy at a bar checking out the lady bartender. I bought it and took it to my table. I wrote:

Dear Margaret,

I guess I'm in cowboy country now. We're still three hours from Pendleton and Kevin hasn't got us kicked out yet. I will send you some more postcards when I get there.

Pete.

Kevin came up behind me and read it over my shoulder. "Dude, who's Margaret?"

"Nobody," I said, covering what I had written.

"What? Is she your girlfriend?"

"Kinda."

"What do you mean, 'kinda'? When did this happen?"

"Two weeks ago."

"Are you serious?" he said excitedly. He took the seat next to mine. "What have you guys done so far?"

"Nothing much. Made out."

"Dude. That's awesome. What's her name? What's she look like?"

I told him.

"I know that girl. Yeah, she's cool."

"You think?"

"Well, she's your girlfriend, don't *you* think?"

"I guess so."

"And she's smart. Yeah, Margaret. Kinda pudgy. She's like the artsy poetry chick."

"Since when are you into poetry?" I said.

"I'm into whatever. I like chicks that go for stuff. Whatever they're into, as long as they're into it all the way. You know?" His eyes got shiny with excitement. "Like this girl I met last summer. Did I tell you about her? She used to hang out at Barnes and Noble, always writing in her journal and reading sex books. Like *erotic literature* from France. Those kinda chicks are the best. And they'll do stuff. Like right away, if they're into you."

I thought about Margaret in this light. It didn't make me like her more. Did she read sex books from France? I hoped not.

In Pendleton we got our rooms at the hotel and then went swimming in the hotel pool. That was pretty fun. The other cute girl in jazz band, besides Pam Olson, was Jennifer Buckmeyer. She came swimming with us. Kevin immediately told her I had a girlfriend.

"*You* have a girlfriend?" said Jennifer. She had never really noticed me before, but now she swam right up to me. "Peter has a girlfriend? Oh my God, that is so cute!" She wanted to know who it was and what she was like. It was hard talking to her, especially face-to-face with her in a swimsuit. She had one of the best bodies in our school.

+++

Kevin and I shared a room. Later we got Cokes from the vending machine, and Kevin made us rum and Cokes with some rum he had smuggled in. We drank them and played cards and watched Motocross on ESPN. Kevin thought he should sneak over to Jennifer Buckmeyer's room to see what she was doing. He thought she had flirted with him in the pool. Did I think she liked him?

I didn't know. Then Kevin complained how boring jazz band had become. When he was a freshman they had snuck out of the hotel and partied in the park across the highway. People had hooked up. No one was doing anything fun this time.

It was true, but I was happy anyway. To me this was the life: chilling in a hotel room, a big gig the next day. The best part was thinking about Margaret. I still couldn't quite believe it: *I had a girlfriend*. She was waiting for me back home. She was probably thinking about me, probably right at that moment. And I was thinking about her.

★★★ **13** ★★★

Saturday morning was the first round of the competition. We were terrible. Everything went wrong. Pam screwed up. Kevin screwed up. Our best soloist, this tall guy named Brandon Hughes who played trombone, even messed up.

Nobody cared though. It was a hundred degrees outside, and as soon as we were done we all hurried back to the hotel and tore off our clothes and ran to the pool.

Later that afternoon, I walked into town and got another postcard for Margaret. I went into a McDonald's and wrote:

Dear Margaret,
    Did you get my other postcard yet? We lost the competition. We would probably come in last if the rankings went down that far. Last night we swam and hung out in our hotel room. Okay bye.
Pete.

That night Brandon and Jennifer Buckmeyer came to our hotel room. And then Pam Olson came and a freshman guy named Steve. We drank rum and Cokes to celebrate how much we sucked.

Jennifer wanted to go skinny-dipping. I didn't see how they could—the pool was closed. Kevin, naturally, was all for it. He was the only volunteer though, so he and Jennifer went by themselves. The rest of us tried to act casual as they ran down the stairs in their swimsuits. I guess they took them off in the pool. I don't know. The pool light was off, so you couldn't see anyway.

That kind of ended the party for everyone else. Pam and Brandon went back to their rooms. Steve the freshman wanted to hang out, but I told him I had to sleep. When he was gone I clicked on MTV. I thought about Margaret. I found myself talking to her in my head. A band would come on and I would tell her stuff about them, like what kind of guitars they had, or what harmonies they were doing, or something they were doing wrong.

A little while later Kevin came back. He was very excited. He started putting on his clothes.

"Now what are you doing?" I asked him.

"Me and Jennifer are going to walk around," he said. "We're going to check out the park."

"Oh," I said.

"Dude, watch my back. You know, if Mr. Moran comes."

"He won't come."

"I know," he said, buttoning his shirt. "Hey, wish me luck."

"Good luck," I said. I heard Jennifer whisper something as he went outside. They both giggled and disappeared. I lay back. I thought about Margaret more. I wondered if she read sex books. I hoped she didn't. I didn't know anything about sex, and how embarrassing would that be? I thought about calling her and asking her, but even if she did, what could I do about it? She was going to be smarter than me about a lot of things. I would just have to deal with it.

The next day we drove home. Kevin and I sat together, and he asked me about Mad Skillz. I told him how serious we were as musicians and how fast we could learn songs. We could practically learn them off the radio. I told him how much money we got for different kinds of dances and how making money made you a professional and that was a different vibe from something like jazz band or jamming in someone's basement. It felt different. It was serious.

He told me about the band he was in with Billy and Nick Carlisle. They were still learning to play their guitars but they were improving really fast. The problem was the bass player kept flaking out.

"What kind of music is it?" I asked.

Kevin got very excited. "It's like heavy metal riffs mixed with punk mixed with like, surf music."

"That sounds weird," I said. "What songs do they play?"

"They write their own songs."

"How can they write their own songs," I said, "if they're still learning to play their instruments?"

"It's better actually. It keeps things simple. And you can rock out. I mean, these guys *rock out*. And girls come over. Seriously, just to watch the practice. They got these two girls from Bradley Day School. Chelsea and Kim. And these girls are *seriously* hot."

Kevin sat back. A big smile spread over his face as he imagined it. For Kevin that was the ultimate selling point of a band. Did you get chicks?

I remained unimpressed. Later Kevin was still talking about it. "No, it's awesome man, I'm telling you. These guys are going places. Billy and Nick, they're for real."

★ ★ ★ 14 ★ ★ ★

The last day of school was June 10. It was a typical last day of school. People were running around, signing yearbooks, throwing water balloons in the parking lot. Robert Hatch and a bunch of sophomores were going to Raleigh Park to play Ultimate Frisbee. I wanted to go, but those guys were like, *Don't you have to hang out with Margaret?* I guessed I did, but I really wanted to play Ultimate. It was the only sport I was halfway good at.

At fifth period Margaret came to my locker and I told her about Raleigh Park. She said she could go but only if we brought Lauren. I said okay, but later I didn't want to go with them. I mean, it was nothing against them, I just wanted to play Ultimate for a few hours and not have to deal with her and Lauren. By that point I had hung out with Margaret every day for two weeks.

So I told her I had to go home and made an excuse about helping my dad. I snuck around and met Robert Hatch in the parking lot and went to the park with them. But only five people showed up to play Ultimate. It wasn't even that fun, and I felt guilty the whole time.

That night I called Margaret.

"Did you help your dad?" she asked me.

"Kind of . . . actually . . . there's something. . . ."

"Did you go to the park?" she asked.

"Yeah," I said.

"I thought so," she said.

I was sitting on my bed. I was pulling on a thread on my comforter.

"Was it because of Lauren?" asked Margaret. "Do you not like her?"

"No, she's okay."

"Was it me?"

"No, it was just . . . I just wanted to hang out and play Ultimate."

She didn't say anything.

"It's just, Robert's going to be away all summer," I continued. "I wanted to hang out with him."

Her voice became very quiet. "Do you want to break up?"
she said.

"No. Do you?"

"No."

"Okay," I said.

She didn't talk for a while. "But you lied to me," she said.

"I know. I'm sorry."

"You could have just said something," she said. "It would
have been okay."

"I know," I said. "That's what I should have done."

She didn't talk. I didn't talk.

"I wish you were here," I said. "I miss you."

"I know. Me too."

★ ★ ★ 15 ★ ★ ★

My summer job that year was busing tables at Pedro's, which
was a Denny's-style Mexican restaurant Robert Hatch had
worked at the summer before. Robert had a job at a summer
camp up in the San Juan Islands, so he would be gone until
September.

Busing at Pedro's was hard. You had to bring water to
people and clean tables, and half the time you'd end up running the dishwasher too. Pedro's wasn't a huge corporation,
so at least they didn't have a million rules and regulations.
You could chill when it wasn't too busy. And I only worked
four shifts a week, so it gave me time to practice and hang out.

Margaret and Lauren both had jobs at the mall. Margaret

worked at Nature First, a health food store. Eric and Todd had both graduated, but they were still around, at least for the start of the summer. We had one last Mad Skillz gig at this rich girl's birthday party. We were getting paid $600, so that was good.

During my first couple of weeks at Pedro's, my shift ended at 10 p.m. and I'd ride my bike over to Margaret's and hang out in her basement or whatever. Her mom didn't want me there past eleven, so there wasn't much time. As the nights got warmer though, we hung out at Lauren's house, sitting on her front lawn. Lauren liked a guy named Travis who worked at the mall. So Margaret and I would hang out and Lauren would talk about Travis.

The birthday party gig was on June 23. Margaret and Lauren were coming, so that was a big deal, her actually seeing me play.

It was a really fun gig. The girl had a huge backyard and they set up a big stage for us. We started playing while the sun was still up. Eric and Todd both wore sunglasses. Margaret was enjoying it too. She sat in the grass and watched and nodded her head to the beat. Lauren talked to Todd Harrison during a break. He seemed to like her at first but later ignored her. He did that to girls a lot.

Afterward, the girl's dad paid us in cash. Eric deducted various stuff and gave us our cut, $90 each. Todd didn't think that was enough. Eric reminded him about renting the PA and putting some in the band fund and all that. Todd thought we should get more. He kept arguing until Eric got pissed too. It seemed like they might actually start fighting. Then Todd

40

yanked his amplifier out of the back of Eric's van and carried it to his pickup. He got his guitar and threw that in his pickup too.

Eric stood there watching him. Daniel too. "We've always done the split this way," Eric said to me. "What's his problem?" The problem was that Eric and Todd had both graduated. Eric, as usual, had a million plans. He wanted to continue Mad Skillz next year. He was also giving guitar lessons and was starting a guitar-lesson Web site. He had enrolled for summer classes at Portland State and was getting a teaching certificate.

Todd wasn't doing anything. He didn't have any plans. He wasn't going to college, he didn't have a job. Still, that was no reason to get pissed at Eric. Or the rest of us. *We* didn't do anything. It was weird to see him so upset. He was always Mr. Cool. He got in his truck and slammed the door and drove away.

"Haven't I always done the splits this way?" Eric asked us.

"Whatever," said Daniel. "That guy bugs me anyway."

That night Lauren's parents were gone, and we went to her house and drank some beer her brother had. Lauren drank quite a bit and called Travis. A girl at the mall had told her to do this. When Travis answered, the first thing Lauren said was, "I'm kind of drunk." Margaret and I watched TV while this was happening.

The rest of the phone call didn't go well. It lasted about thirty seconds. When Lauren hung up she was totally embarrassed. She started crying. It was a big disaster, and I eventually had to leave her and Margaret alone.

★★★ 16 ★★★

For Fourth of July, my dad took me and Margaret and Lauren to this special place he knew about on the Columbia River to watch the fireworks. It was somebody's family farm, an old musician friend. We parked in a big field with a bunch of other cars. There was a big bonfire, and everyone played their car stereos and drank keg beer. It was a pretty wild scene. Lauren thought it was cool that my dad liked to party. That always happened. Other kids always liked my dad because he didn't seem like a real dad.

The next day I had work at noon. Kevin called me just as I was walking out the door. I was surprised to hear from him, I never really talked to him outside school.

"Hey, what are you doing?" he said.

"Nothing," I said. "How's Jennifer Buckmeyer?"

"She's great. She's my girlfriend now."

"For real?"

"Totally for real. How's Margaret?"

"She's good."

"Hey listen, the reason I called, you know my band? With the Carlisle brothers? We need a bass player."

"Oh," I said. I had thought this might happen. I had already made up my mind not to get involved with the Carlisle brothers.

"You interested?"

"Uh . . ." I said.

"What's Mad Skillz doing these days?" he asked

"We're kind of done for the summer."

"Yeah? So you have time, perfect."

"But you guys are like . . . you're more like a jam band right? You just play riffs and stuff."

"Yeah, but it rocks. Billy Carlisle, he's unbelievable."

"How so?"

"He just goes for it. He puts it all out there."

"What does that mean?"

"He's like, he's the real deal."

I didn't say anything. I didn't want to insult anyone. "I know it's probably great, but you know me. I've been playing since I was five. I can't play some three-note riff over and over."

"It's not about that. It's about the power of it. It's about the energy."

"What kind of energy?"

"I can't explain it to you. You just gotta play with us. Come on Saturday. I told them about you. They want to meet you."

That night, Margaret and I hung out at Lauren's. Margaret and Lauren were talking about Travis. Lauren said how lucky me and Margaret were, to be together and to have each other.

Afterward, walking Margaret back to her house I told her about Kevin and the Carlisle brothers. I told her I had turned them down.

"Why?" she said, surprised. "You're not doing anything now."

"Yeah, but they're not real musicians."

"Have you actually seen them play?"

"No," I said. "But I've heard stuff about them."

"Like what?" said Margaret.

"They're the Carlisle brothers. They're party guys. They went to Bradley Day School."

"So?"

"They're probably just rich kids goofing around."

"Well, if you don't want to . . ." she said. "That seems strange though. I thought you liked Kevin. I thought you guys were friends."

I talked to my dad.

"I always like playing with new people," he said. "You might learn something. And if you don't, it's just one rehearsal."

"They're not very serious. It sounds like they barely know how to play."

"Well, you've had an advantage in that way, being in this family. Not everyone is going to be as advanced as you are."

"They live in Clairmont," I said.

"Clairmont's a nice neighborhood."

"They're probably just rich kids goofing around."

"You never know," said my dad. "Until you go see."

★ ★ ★ **17** ★ ★ ★

I went to the Carlisles' house on Saturday. It was a big two-story house. The grass was freshly cut, and there were sprinklers going on the lawn. Their dad answered the front door. He was well dressed, like a businessman on the weekend. He walked me through their kitchen to the door that led to the basement. He joked that he was leaving the house before the "awful racket" began.

I carried my bass to the basement. Kevin was waiting for me at the bottom of the stairs. He introduced me to Nick Carlisle, a tall, good-looking guy but with enough scruffiness that you knew he was into music. I looked around at their equipment. It was an odd combinations of things, Marshall Heads on top of HiWatt speakers, that sort of thing. It was all good stuff. It was not cheap. So that was good.

Then Billy Carlisle came down the stairs. He was shorter than his brother, short and wiry. He had long hair that hung in his face. Unlike his brother, he didn't smile.

"Hi," I said to him.

He stared at me.

Kevin introduced us from behind the drums. "Pete this is Billy. Billy, Pete. Pete here is probably the best pure musician we've got at Evergreen. He's in Mad Skillz with Eric Simon."

Billy flipped his hair out of his face. He stared at me. "What kind of bass you got?" he finally said. I opened my case and showed him my Fender Precision, which is generally considered the best rock bass in the world.

He glanced at it. "Are those good?" he said.

It took a while to tune up and get everything ready. They had a microphone and speakers so Nick could sing. When Billy turned up his guitar volume I knew their father wasn't kidding. This was going to be very loud. Kevin played an intro on the drums, and the three of them started bashing away. It was a god-awful noise, mostly an E chord, with some stray notes thrown in. I did my best to join in. I played along, playing a steady E at first, then moving around, filling in the space, jamming on it.

Billy instantly stopped. Everyone else stopped. He stared at me. "We don't really play that kind of style," he said.

"What kind of style?" I said, staring back at him. The Carlisle brothers might have been older than me, but they were rank amateurs. I wasn't taking any crap.

"You know," he said, pointing at my fingers. "What you're doing. Playing all that extra stuff."

"What extra stuff? I'm just playing."

"We don't do that."

"What am I supposed to play?" I said.

"Something simple."

"That was simple."

"No it wasn't."

"Well," I said, looking hard into his face. "What do you want me to play?"

"Something cool," said Billy. "Something low and hard."

Nick interrupted. "Why don't we play through the whole song first," he said. "And he can see where the different parts are. He can see what we're looking for."

So they did that. I stood and watched. They played the same E chord for a while, bashing away like insane people, then Nick screamed into the microphone for a few bars, then they started bashing again. It was ridiculous. It was a joke.

"That's it?" I said, when they finished. "That's your song?"

"What's wrong with it?" said Billy, glaring at me.

"It's *one chord*," I said, glaring right back.

"What kind of songs do you like?"

"Songs that have more than one chord?"

"Let's forget it," said Billy, turning away. "This guy isn't going to work."

Kevin spoke up. "You guys, give him a break. He's good, just let him play. He'll figure it out."

"What kind of music do you like?" said Billy, turning toward me again.

"Good music," I said. Billy was really getting on my nerves.

He named some obscure bands. Had I heard of them? I hadn't. "This isn't going to work," he said, again. "Sorry man, no offense. I'm sure you're great at your thing but this is something totally different."

"Yeah and what sort of thing is that?" I replied. "People who can't even play? People who can only play E major seven?"

Billy smiled. "Is that what that is? E major seven?"

Nick laughed nervously. "E major seven, well now we know."

Kevin was still worried though. "Dudes, we have gigs. We

need a bass player. Just let him play. He's smart. He'll figure it out."

They did. They played three more songs. I joined in occasionally, but it was hard to know what to do.

When we'd all had enough, Nick took off his guitar and ran upstairs. He came back with a CD. It was a practice recording they had done with their old bass player. "You wouldn't have to play exactly what he played," he told me quietly, so Billy wouldn't hear. "If you could just do something, you know, with less notes."

I felt so insulted I almost didn't take it. But something made me. Maybe it was because my dad had once said the exact same thing. "That's good," he had told me, "now do it with less notes."

★★★ 18 ★★★

That night my dad had a gig and Margaret came to my house. Her parents didn't like her coming over, so she told them she was at Lauren's. We made out in my room most of the night. It got pretty intense, like not actually having sex but most everything else. Afterward we were walking around half naked and eating stuff and goofing around in the kitchen.

Then I took her into the living room and showed her the Carlisle brothers' CD. "Check this crap out," I told her, putting it on. Margaret kneeled on the floor and listened. The first song started. She nodded her head in time.

"Isn't it terrible?" I said.

"It's not *terrible*. . . ."

"Listen to this part," I said. "They can't even change chords together."

Margaret listened. She was doing what all nonmusicians do, she was listening to the vocals. On the first song there was an actual melody. It was only a couple of notes, but it was enough to make it seem like a real song.

"I kind of like it," said Margaret. "They wrote this themselves?"

"You just like the words," I said. I punched forward to the next song. It was called "Girl in the Window." I remembered it from practice. It had a catchy bass line that even their terrible bass player could manage. Margaret immediately began to bounce to it.

Nick sang:

Girl in the window
Girl passing by
Waiting for her friends to come
Waiting for someone
To show her the sky

"This one's pretty good," said Margaret. "Don't you think?"

"No," I said, angrily. "It's not good. It's barely a song. It's one riff."

"I don't care. I like it."

I turned down the stereo. I went into the other room and brought back my bass. I played the riff on my bass. "See? It's just the same thing over and over. And the guy can barely play it."

49

"But it's catchy," she said. "And it makes you want to dance."

"But it's just one thing, over and over."

Margaret looked at me. "Why do you hate them so much?" she said. "Just because you're a better musician doesn't mean they're not good in their way."

I turned off the CD. I took my bass back to my room. Margaret was standing up when I returned. She was going to be late. She had to get home.

At the door she tried to kiss me, but I didn't want to. I didn't see how she could like the Carlisle brothers' band.

"Peter, you can't be mad because I liked some of their songs," she said, on my front step.

"They're terrible though. And they think they're so great."

"You're the one who thinks you're so great," she said. "Your ego is too big."

"*My* ego is too big? What about *their* egos? They're the ones—"

"With music you think you know everything. You're afraid to try something new."

"I'm not afraid. That's ridiculous. I can play every kind of music. I can play jazz, blues, country."

"Then why can't you give them a chance?"

"Because they're *amateurs*," I said. "How am I supposed to play with people who don't know what they're doing?"

"Maybe they know some things."

"What could they know?"

"They know how to have fun for one thing," said Margaret. "They know how to express themselves."

"I know how to have fun," I said. "Music isn't always about fun."

"What is it about then?" she said.

"It's about other things. Things I can't explain."

She didn't answer. "Will you kiss me at least?" she said.

I kissed her once. On the cheek.

"That's it?"

"That's all I feel like right now," I said.

She watched my face. She was searching for something. She didn't find it. "Okay," she said finally. She walked down the steps. "Bye."

"Bye," I said.

★★★ **19** ★★★

Kevin came to Pedro's. It was a slow night, and he found me reading *Bass Player* magazine in the kitchen. I was wearing the apron they make you wear.

"Nice apron," he said.

"Thanks," I said.

He leaned up against the wall and jammed his hands in his pockets. "What'd you think of that practice CD?"

"I thought it sucked."

"Dude, it doesn't suck," he said calmly. "You might not like it, but it doesn't suck."

"I don't like it and it sucks."

"It kicks ass and you know it."

"And worst of all," I said, "worst of all . . ."

"What?"

"Margaret and I got in a fight about it."

"See? *See?* She liked it right? Chicks dig that stuff. Chicks know what's up. They can feel the energy."

"Bad playing does not equal energy."

"Dude, you're not hearing it. I swear, you got some blockage thing happening. It rocks. I'm telling you."

"I hold them responsible. I hold *you* responsible."

"For what?"

"For my fight with Margaret." I tossed the magazine down and looked around the restaurant for dishes to bus.

"Have you learned the songs?" asked Kevin.

"No, I haven't learned the songs."

"Have you learned some of them?"

"I could play all those songs in my sleep, okay?" I said.

"So you'll come practice with us tomorrow?"

"No, I will not come practice with you tomorrow."

"Why not?"

"Because I'm not going to be in this band," I said.

"Can you just do it as a favor? We have gigs. We're supposed to play next week."

"Where?"

"This place downtown. It's an all-ages show. It's going to be awesome."

"Yeah?" I said. I was a little surprised they actually had a gig. "What sort of place is it?"

"It's a club. They have a huge stage, a sound system, stage lights, the whole deal."

"Have you been there?"

"Sure. We played the last one. All these cool people show up. All these downtown people."

"Really? What's it called."

"Sanctuary," said Kevin. He was getting that shiny excited look in his eyes. "They have a sound man. The same guy who does the real bands when they come through. They do effects on the vocals. They reverb the snare drum. It's top-of-the-line, all the way."

I thought about this. It was shocking. The Carlisle brothers were going to play in a real club? When Mad Skillz had never played anything but dances?

"How much do you get paid?" I asked, wiping my hands on my apron.

"Not much. I think we got forty bucks last time."

"See!" I said. "See! That's what you get. People aren't going to pay to see a band that can't play. Forty bucks! What a joke!"

"Dude, who cares?" said Kevin. "There's chicks. It's fun. And you can party with the other bands." His voice lowered, "And it's true, you know, *what they say.*"

"Yeah?" I said. "What do they say?"

"Playing live." He grinned. "It's better than sex."

"Nothing's better than sex," I said.

"Yeah?" he said. "Really? So you and Margaret . . . ?"

I shook my head. "No, we haven't, but I'm sure it's better than playing one-chord songs to a bunch of downtown weirdos."

★★★ **20** ★★★

"Kevin said it was better than sex," I told Margaret. We had made up from our fight. We lay on our sides on Lauren's lawn. Lauren was talking to Travis on her cell phone.

"What was?" Margaret asked.

"Playing this all-ages show downtown."

"Was it called Sanctuary?" she said.

I looked up. "Yeah. How did you know?"

"This girl at the mall was talking about it."

"What did she say?"

"She said she and her friends have gone a couple times."

"Yeah?" I said, picking at the grass.

"She loves it," said Margaret. "Her friend is in a band."

"Would you want to go to something like that?"

"Sure, why not?"

I picked at the grass some more.

Lauren hung up the phone. "Oh my God!" she squealed.

"What did he say?" asked Margaret.

"He said his friend has a pool and a bunch of people are going to hang out tomorrow night."

"That's great!" said Margaret.

"You guys have to go with me though," said Lauren.

"I have to work," I said.

"I can't," said Margaret. "I have to babysit for the Rosenbergs."

"I can't go by myself!" said Lauren. "Please. Margaret you have to."

"You can go by yourself," said Margaret.

"But I'll have to wear a *bathing suit*," pleaded Lauren.

"You're going to have to wear one sometime. It's summer."

"But he's going to hate my body!"

"He's not going to hate your body," said Margaret. "Guys like skinny girls. Right, Pete? Models are skinny."

I shrugged. I was thinking about Sanctuary. I was thinking about gigs that were better than sex.

"Just go," Margaret told her.

"You have to go," repeated Lauren. "If you don't, I'm not going."

"Who else is going to be there?" asked Margaret.

"Lots of people. Brian from the mall."

"Brian from Footlocker?"

"Yeah. He's nice. You said so yourself. Will you come? *Please?*"

"I don't know. Maybe I can come after."

I walked Margaret back to her house.

"So you're not going to help Kevin?" said Margaret.

"Help him? You mean play in his band? No. I already told him."

"But you would be helping him. I mean, he obviously wants to play at that place."

"They can get someone else for that."

"Can they though? It sounds like they need you."

"They're not going to get me," I said.

"But you're only thinking about it in terms of the music. You could also think of it as, Kevin's your friend and he needs your help."

"I don't see it like that."

"I know you don't," she said. "That's what I'm saying. Maybe you should."

We arrived at her driveway. We stopped. "Why are we talking about this again? It's not that big of an issue. I don't like their music. What's so hard to understand about that?"

"I'm just saying he's your friend."

"Oh brother," I said. "You know what? You would be a lot better girlfriend if you would stop telling me what to do all the time."

"Sorry. God. I'm just trying to help."

"Well it's not helping," I said. I turned and walked away. Without kissing her. Without saying good-bye. I glanced back and she was still standing there, watching me. I didn't care. I kept walking.

★★★ 21 ★★★

The next day I woke up earlier than usual. I lay in my bed and thought about Margaret. Why did she keep getting in fights with me? I rolled over. The clock radio had turned on in my dad's room. The traffic and weather was blasting. He must not have come home. I thought about him with a woman somewhere, waking up with her lying beside him. What would that be like, waking up with your girlfriend right next to you?

I got up and made something to eat. I thought more about Margaret. What if she broke up with me? What if she went home last night, unkissed, and said, *Screw this guy*? I didn't have to be at Pedro's until later. I decided to go see her at work. I would tell her I was sorry, or at least tell her something.

Outside it was hot. I got my bike from the garage and rode to the mall. It was air-conditioned inside and not too crowded, since it was still early. I was walking down the main concourse when I spotted Margaret and Lauren, sipping smoothies in the lower food court. They were at a table with two guys. One of them was Travis. The other was someone I didn't know, probably Brian from Footlocker who I'd heard about.

I stopped when I saw them. I stayed where I was, out of sight. They were all laughing about something. Margaret most of all. She said something, and they all laughed again. Travis and Brian were standard mall types, good-looking, trendy. Brian wore those new retro Nikes. Travis wore a blue suit coat with little punk buttons on it.

They were going swimming later, I remembered. I moved to a post and stood behind it. I watched Margaret. She looked different for some reason. She was so relaxed and happy. She was talking again, telling Brian something. Her face rose and fell with the story. The two boys listened eagerly as she talked. They hung on her every word.

Margaret. It hit me all at once: she was so much cuter than I thought. She was so much cooler than I knew. I had undervalued her. I had underestimated her—all because the people at school had made fun of her. I watched her laughing and talking and sipping her smoothie. Travis and Brian were as cool as anyone at Evergreen, *and they adored her*. Brian definitely liked her. It was so obvious. And she liked him, from the looks of it. And later she would be half naked in his pool, they would all be . . .

That part hit me too. It hit me hard. I snuck away. I went back and got my bike.

Riding back, I kind of lost my mind. I got totally paranoid. I talked myself into a frenzy. At my house, I threw my bike down in the yard and went inside. I slammed the door and went to the phone. I was going to call Margaret. I was going to break up with her. She obviously liked Brian. He was obviously more her type. Why was she even going out with someone like me? For that matter why didn't she just go out with the Carlisle brothers since she liked *them* so much?

I grabbed the phone. I punched in her number at Nature First. Margaret answered. She said, "Nature First, how can I help you?"

She sounded so normal. Like she always did. It made me hesitate. "Margaret?" I said.

"Peter, hey, what's up?"

"Nothing I just. I was just . . ."

"Oh my God. That's so funny. We were just talking about you at lunch."

"Who was?"

"Lauren and Travis and Brian."

"Yeah . . . ? What were you saying?"

"Just how at first you thought I was weird."

"Oh."

"Do you remember that first time we talked? You thought I was so weird."

"I never thought you were weird," I said, weakly.

"Yes, you did," she said. "Remember? When we went to the mall? You didn't even want to sit with me on the bus."

"It's just sometimes when I ride the bus with Robert we sit in different seats and put our feet up."

"It doesn't matter," she said. "I don't care."

I swallowed. "Are you still going swimming with those guys?"

"No. Brian has to go somewhere with his girlfriend. Travis and Lauren are going to the movies. So that's probably better anyway. If I don't have to babysit, I'd rather hang out with you."

"Yeah?" I said, trying to process all this information.

"I mean, if you want to."

"No," I said. "I want to. I was just. I was thinking about last night—"

"Oh my God. Last night. I'm *so sorry*. That was totally my fault. I shouldn't tell you what to do. Travis and Brian even said so. Especially about your music . . ."

"No, but you were right—"

"Oops, I have a customer," whispered Margaret. "So we'll meet later?"

"Yeah."

"I'll see you then."

"Margaret?"

"Yeah?"

"I like you so much," I blurted. "I do. I know I was hesitating at first. But I do. I swear. If you ever broke up with me . . ."

"Oh my God. Peter. That's so sweet. Me too. I have to go. I'll see you tonight."

I hung up the phone. I sat in a chair and took a deep breath. Margaret Little. I loved her. It was so weird.

A minute later I called Kevin. I asked him if they still needed a bass player.

"Yeah, totally," he said. "I mean, were you thinking you might . . . ?"

"I'll do it," I said. "I'm in."

★★★ 22 ★★★

"When you're first starting you might as well try a lot of things," my dad said, when I told him I was joining up with the Carlisle Brothers (for the summer anyway). We were eating dinner. I had made hamburgers. That was my new thing I was learning to make. The cook at Pedro's had been giving me tips, like put a little onion in the meat before you cook it.

"I remember auditioning with this terrible New Wave band in the eighties," said my dad. "These guys were hilarious. They were basically a bar band, but they heard the Huey Lewis and the News record and they figured if Huey could do it, so could they."

My hamburger was falling apart. I would have to ask the cook about that.

"I mean, this was the *early* eighties," said my dad. "I wasn't much older than you." His hamburger was falling apart too. He ate it anyway. "So I went to meet with them and they had their little New Wave outfits. They couldn't finish a song without stopping to talk about how huge New Wave was going to be."

"They were trying to cash in," I said.

"It was all based on Huey Lewis," said my dad. "And they couldn't waste one second. They had to act now. The Huey Lewis New Wave train was leaving the station. And they had to get on."

"Man," I said, chewing my hamburger.

"They had one song." My dad was chewing too. "I still remember it, it was called "'You're My Baby.'" They thought it was the greatest song ever written. They were sure it would be a number one hit. The only problem was, was it New Wave enough? Was it *Huey* enough?"

"How long did you stay with them?"

"A couple rehearsals. I couldn't take it, but I always worried one day I'd be driving somewhere and 'You're My Baby' would come on the radio."

I licked my fingers and got a paper towel from the roll. My dad was picking hamburger bits out of his lap and eating them. We lived a bachelor life.

"Years later I saw one of them," he said. "He had become a high school science teacher. He seemed happy enough."

"That's hilarious," I said. I wadded up my paper towel and shot it at the trash can across the kitchen. It banked off the toaster and went in. "What did Mom think of them?"

"I never told your mom about those guys. I would have been too embarrassed."

"She was too cool for stuff like that, huh?"

"She was kind of . . . serious. I don't mean without a

sense of humor, but she didn't suffer fools very well."

"You think she would have been big?" I asked.

"She would have been *huge* . . ." he said without think-ing. Then he paused, and shrugged. "I don't know. I always say that. Who knows. It's a tough business. . . ."

I nodded. I picked a bit of onion from my own lap and chewed it thoughtfully.

★ ★ ★ **23** ★ ★ ★

On Saturday afternoon I was back in the Carlisles' basement.

"Okay," said Nick when we were plugged in and ready to go. Billy Carlisle took a deep swig of a Coke he had on his amp. He still seemed skeptical of my abilities, but they had no choice at this point.

We started the first song. I played the parts the way they were on the CD. Nothing fancy. Afterward, Billy looked over and nodded at me. "That sounds good," he said.

I played the next song the same way. Simple. Big. Heavy. That's what they wanted, that's what they got. It was kind of fun in a way. I'd never played anything so raw and aggressive before. There was a definite power to it.

After a couple of songs, Billy had to tune up again. As we waited, there was a noise above us and the excited sound of several people running down the stairs. It was Jennifer Buckmeyer, and two other girls. When Jennifer saw me she squealed with delight. "Oh my God, it's Peter from jazz band," she said. "Look how cute he is!" She kissed me on the cheek.

I blushed terribly. She ran over and kissed Kevin.

"We're kind of in the middle of practice," he whispered to her.

"That's okay, we won't bug you."

Kevin introduced the other girls. Their names were Chelsea and Kim. They were the Bradley Day School girls Kevin had talked about. They looked kind of young to be hanging out with Nick and Billy, who were nineteen and twenty-one, respectively. They sat on the old couch. Jennifer went to the fridge by the stairs and got everyone Cokes.

We started "Girl in the Window," the song with the cool bass line. I don't know what kind of crappy instrument their old bass player had, but I had a Fender Precision. When I played the riff, the whole room seemed to swing with it. Also, as Kevin and I fell into the groove of it, we added a little hitch. We put in one tiny stutter note—it was a trick we'd learned in jazz band. It sounded amazing. Nick and Billy both grinned with approval.

The girls loved it too. They all bobbed their heads on the couch. When we finished, the three of them clapped. "That is the best song!" said Kim.

"That was awesome!" said Jennifer.

It *was* awesome. I wanted to play it again. I asked Kevin if we could, but Nick said no, we didn't have time. We had to keep going.

That night my dad was gone and Margaret came over. We made out in my bed. Things got very intense. We got totally naked and did things we had never done before. We were getting very close to doing "it." We were running out of other things to do.

After that, we went into my backyard and snuggled under a blanket and watched the stars. All night, I had been telling her about the practice. How fun it was, how cool it was, but how I still considered the Carlisle brothers to be amateurs. It was more like a fun summer project, something to say you did. Like one day I would tell my kids about the Carlisle brothers the same way my dad told me about the Huey Lewis guys.

"What's the name of their band?" Margaret asked me.

"Probably something weird," I said. "They said one of the bands we're playing with is called The Idiots."

★ ★ ★ 24 ★ ★ ★

The name of our band was The Tiny Masters of Today. Kevin told me this as he drove me home after another quick practice.

It was the middle of July now, and the night was hot. I was riding with the window open, my hand out the window. "What's that supposed to mean?" I said.

"It's a Nietzsche quote. You know, the German guy. The one who said what doesn't kill you makes you stronger."

"Huh," I said.

"Yeah," said Kevin. "I guess it's philosophy or something. It means people who have authority, like teachers and cops."

"Huh," I said again. I was trying to imagine it on a marquee. It was awfully long.

64

"I guess that's what it means," said Kevin. "That's what Billy said."

"Why do people always have to attack authority?" I said.

"It's the thing to do."

"I mean, what are teachers supposed to do?" I said. "*Not* make you study? Or cops? Would you want them to *not* arrest people who are stealing your stuff?"

"No, I guess not," said Kevin. "But authority sucks. I mean, you don't have it that bad. You just have your dad, and he's cool."

I watched out the window.

"I don't know what the name means," said Kevin. "Maybe they just like the sound of it."

"I don't know about those guys," I said.

"Yeah, but it's fun though, right? You see what I'm talking about?"

"Yeah, I guess."

The Saturday night before the gig I went with Margaret to a movie at the mall. It was hard to stay focused though. I was really nervous, way more than I had been for any Mad Skillz gig, even the Spring Dance. With those, you knew what it was going to be. With this, I had no idea.

After the movie I drove us to Raleigh Park and we walked around in the grass and found a place at the edge of the trees to lie down. We made out for a while and then we lay on our back and stared at the night sky. I tried to picture what Sanctuary would look like. I kept thinking of places I had seen my dad play, blues clubs, jazz clubs, but those were full of old people. Sanctuary would be full of young people. That was the part I couldn't picture.

I turned toward Margaret, but her head was turned slightly away from me. I propped myself up so I could see her better but she turned her head away more.

"Margaret?" I said.

"Yeah."

"Are you all right?"

"Yeah."

"Sorry I keep spacing out."

"It's okay. You're nervous," she said. Her hand found my forearm. She squeezed it.

"I know. I totally am." I picked at the grass. I picked until I had a handful, then I threw it at my feet.

"It's okay," she said again.

I smoothed the grass with my fingers. The summer moon was shining through the trees across from us. "You know . . . I love you," I said.

She didn't move. "I love you too," she said quietly.

I smoothed the grass. Crickets were chirping in the woods. I scooted closer to her. Her head was still turned away. I touched her hair with my fingertips. I touched the side of her face. I lifted my head and kissed her forehead, her eyebrows, the bridge of her nose.

"Do you think we should have sex?" she said suddenly.

I pulled back slightly. "Sure," I said. "If you do. I mean, when you're ready." I went back to kissing her face.

"When do you think we should?" she said.

"Whenever," I said. "When do you think you'll want to?"

"I don't know," she said, but her body tensed up. Her breathing changed slightly.

I pulled back more. "You don't mean like . . . do you mean like . . . *now*?"

She didn't say anything. Her chest heaved.

"Like here? Outside?"

She didn't say anything. She didn't have to. I was up and running, to my dad's car. I had a condom in the side door compartment, hidden in a box of Band-Aids. . . .

The Tiny Masters
of Today

in
the
inside.
the door.

etty
ike the

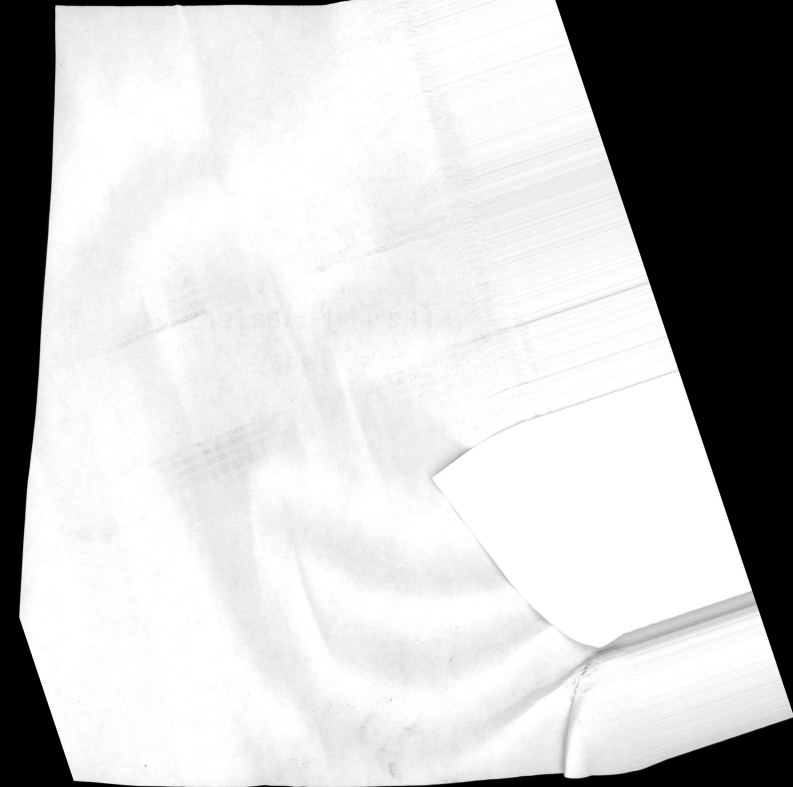

The Tiny Masters
of Today

★★★ **25** ★★★

I rode to Sanctuary with Kevin. Nick and Billy were ahead of us in their mom's minivan. Kevin had a CD playing in the car stereo; it was one of his noisy underground bands. I sat in the passenger seat. Out my window was the normal, day-lit world, the world of cars and families and Sunday dinners. The Tiny Masters of Today somehow went against all that. *I* was now going against all that.

We pulled up in front of the club. Sanctuary was a grim, windowless building with metal bars on the front door. It was painted black. The Carlisle brothers parked their minivan in front of us. Nick Carlisle walked to the door and banged on it through the bars. Someone opened it and talked to him. We would have to wait, the club wasn't open yet. Kevin parked and stood on the sidewalk and joked nervously about a bum who was sleeping in a doorway across the street.

Jennifer Buckmeyer pulled up. I was always glad to see her. She had brought Kevin's favorite shirt. She was pretty dressed up herself. She looked like Molly Ringwald, like the eighties mixed with punk mixed with whatever weird stuff she had lying around the house.

I did not have any special clothes. I was wearing jeans and my Reeboks and a shirt I thought would look okay, but once I was standing outside a club downtown, I felt painfully uncool. I whispered to Kevin asking if I could wear the Buzzcocks T-shirt he was wearing now, since he was going to change into the shirt Jennifer brought. He said I could but it might be sweaty.

Another band arrived in a beat-up van. Several tough-looking people staggered out. They wore filthy pants and leather jackets, and there was a woman whose pale white skin looked like it had never seen the light of day. Billy went over to them. Nick whispered to us that they were The Idiots. They were a famous local band. They had been around for years.

Over the next hour, more vans appeared and more musicians. Some people seemed to know one another but in general people were aloof. When they finally unlocked the front door, everyone began moving their equipment inside. As I rolled my bass amp in, I saw a poster tacked on the door. It said:

ALL-AGES EXTRAVAGANZA
Rock on underaged dudes!
Featuring:
The Idiots
Thriftstore Apocalypse
All Girl Summer Fun Band
The Hungry Ghosts

72

The Tiny Masters of Reality
Frumpies
★ July 16 ★ $6.00 ★ All Ages ★ CLUB SANCTUARY ★

"What the—?" said Billy, when he saw the poster. "The Tiny Masters of *Reality*? What the hell is wrong with these people?"

"Come on," said Nick. "It doesn't matter."

I pushed my bass amp into the dark club. The inside of Sanctuary looked like a futuristic haunted house. Everything was black or fluorescent, and there were posters and black lights and stuffed animals hanging from the walls. The stage was in a large room in back. The soundman was there, telling people where to put their equipment. He had long hair, a baseball cap, a leather vest, and a big pocket knife on his belt. He was annoyed to have to accommodate six bands, and he let everyone know. He yelled at a girl who was blocking the stairs with her amp. She couldn't lift it up the steps. Kevin and I ran over and helped her. Nick said she was in the All Girl Summer Fun Band, and they just been written up in *Spin*.

I was like, "*Spin*? The magazine?"

He nodded.

Then a guy carrying a bass knocked into me. He didn't even have a case for his instrument. He was just carrying it like he found it on the street. He wasn't very nice either. He pushed right by me.

There were band people everywhere. There were roadies and friends and girls with leather pants and guys so pale and skinny and dirty they looked half-dead. There were amps and drums and guitars, and a stoner guy on a skateboard crashed into the stage and the sound guy grabbed him and almost

73

punched him out. There was way too much equipment, so the sound guy decided some people would have to share. It got very confusing and complicated.

I tried to keep out of the way, but I couldn't stop staring at everything. Sanctuary was just like Kevin said: a pro sound system, a real stage, real lights, monitors, dressing rooms. I couldn't believe we were going to play there.

★ ★ ★ 26 ★ ★ ★

"Dude, lend me your shirt," I pleaded to Kevin.

"I don't want to change yet," he said. "If you wanted a cool shirt, you should have brought your own."

I turned away impatiently. I needed to wear something that identified me as being in a band. One of the All Girl Summer Fun Band girls had asked me if I was somebody's little brother. Another guy had asked me to get him a Pepsi.

Kevin wouldn't give me his shirt. He and I were standing outside the club. It was still light out at seven. A summer breeze was blowing down the deserted Sunday street.

Nick and Billy came out of the club. Billy was shaking his head. "Bad news," Nick announced. "They're making us go first."

"I thought we were going third," said Kevin.

"They screwed us," said Billy.

"Frumpies cancelled," said Nick. "And The Idiots moved their friends up."

"Can they do that?" said Kevin.

"Of course they can do that," said Billy. "Their drummer books the club."

"We gotta get a manager," said Nick.

"I'll be your manager," said Jennifer Buckmeyer cheerfully. She had appeared behind us.

I grabbed her. "You don't have any other cool shirts do you?"

She thought about it. She ran back to her car and came back with a green T-shirt that said ST. ANNE'S MIDDLE SCHOOL VOLUNTEERS on it. It wasn't the greatest thing, but it was old and worn and better than what I had. I stripped off my shirt and put it on. I was greatly relieved.

I hadn't understood the significance of us playing first when Nick first announced it, but at seven-forty-five, when we stood onstage in front of eight people, I understood. We stalled as long as we could, but the sound guy yelled to us that "the clock was running." Kevin started the first song. Margaret wasn't even there yet. I had told her to come at eight-thirty.

But I didn't have time to think about that. I was too busy being dazzled by the sound system. Every note was crystal clear, every word Nick sang, every chord we played, every crack of Kevin's drums. Also the stage lights made everything look fantastic. My bass sparkled in the spotlight. This was what real bands did. This was why real bands sounded so good.

The first two songs were a blur. I was too nervous to enjoy myself. On "Girl in the Window," I finally managed to relax. The couple of people standing on the outer fringes of the dance floor began bobbing their heads instantly. Jennifer even danced a little by the side of the stage. When the song was over the few people present clapped excitedly. Someone whooped. My heart was racing.

Thirty minutes later we played our last song. By that time, the few audience members present had wandered off. We were literally playing to an empty room.

When the lights came on, there was a mad scramble as the next band hurried onto the stage. I quickly packed my bass and got off. I helped Kevin with his drums and then stood with Jennifer on the side of the stage. Even though no one had seen us, I was totally jacked up. I was so adrenalized my hands were shaking.

Kevin and the Carlisle brothers retreated to the minivan. I stayed by the stage. What were these other bands going to be like? I was very curious.

Next up was The Hungry Ghosts. They were a three-piece. The bass player was a tall, skinny guy in tight red pants. A girl played guitar and sang. There were more girls in down-town bands, I realized. There were never girls in cover bands.

The Hungry Ghosts were going for a frantic, spastic thing. They acted very artsy and aloof. The girl beat on her guitar and stuttered her words while the tall guy stared down at the little group of people who had gathered at the front of the stage. His technique was terrible. He played with a pick, and his bass was cheap and sounded bad. But people still liked them. They clearly had their little gang of followers.

Kevin came back and joined me, sitting on the floor by the stage. The Hungry Ghosts went off and Thriftstore

Apocalypse charged onstage to take their place. They were all dressed like nerdy ten-year-olds. It was fascinating how each group had a special "look" and how they were so determined to be different or unique. They were setting up their stuff when I looked up and saw Margaret and Lauren.

They were very upset. "What happened?" Margaret demanded. "Billy said you already played."

"We had to go first," said Kevin. "They screwed us over."

Margaret stomped her foot. "Why didn't you call me?" she said.

"We didn't have time."

Margaret was mad, but she also couldn't stop looking at the people. Lauren was looking too. They were in shock. They couldn't believe there were so many cool people all in one place.

Margaret sat down on the floor next to me. The club was filling up fast. Margaret, I noticed, was wearing mascara and lipstick and her white headband. That's when I realized I should have worn my red high-tops. They were still stupid, but anything would have been better than the Reeboks I was wearing.

★★★ 27 ★★★

The All Girl Summer Fun Band was next. The place was totally packed when they played. Margaret, Lauren, Kevin, Jenny, and I were all squeezed in by the side of the stage when they played their first song. As advertised, they were five perky college-age girls. They were dressed alternative, but their music style was, as Kevin said, "super simple bubblegum pop." They sang and smiled and were extremely happy about everything—unlike The Hungry Ghosts, who had sneered down at the audience.

But the main thing about the Summer Fun Band was their fans. They were like two hundred of the cutest, hippest girls you ever saw jammed up against the stage. From the minute they started, everyone in the place began bouncing and dancing and singing along. I had assumed all downtown bands had to fit a certain standard of punkness or alternativeness or whatever. But this wasn't punk at all. It wasn't angry or dark. It was total happiness.

The Idiots played last. There were fewer people for them. Their style was more electronic and atmospheric, but they sounded really good and they were dressed to the teeth. The girl wore a silver jumpsuit and tons of makeup and lipstick. The guys were dressed in suits with their dirty hair hanging down and their brooding pale faces squinting in the light.

When it was over, the lights came on. Members of the different bands sorted through the equipment and packed up. Kevin and I stood on the side of the stage watching it all.

"So?" said Kevin. "What do you think?"

"I don't know what to think," I said, honestly enough.

One of the Summer Fun Girls saw us and stopped. "Hey, I liked your band," she said. "What's it called again?"

"The Tiny Masters of Today," said Kevin.

"You guys got that killer instinct," she said and she winked.

"Thanks," said Kevin. She walked away, and Kevin elbowed me. "See what I mean?"

+++

78

Lauren had her car, so I rode home with her and Margaret. I was so drained from everything, I could barely talk. I sat in back and lay across the seat and stared out the window at the streetlights going by.

Lauren dropped off Margaret and me at the top of her street. We walked for a while and then sat on the curb in front of her neighbor's.

"That was *so wild*," I said. "Who were all those people? Where did they come from?"

Margaret dug some Bubblicious out of her pocket. She gave me a piece. I chewed it and stared across the suburban street.

She bumped her knee against my knee. She smiled at me. "So in all the excitement have you forgot what we did last night?"

"No," I said, grinning, "I haven't forgot."

"So?" she said, chewing her gum.

"So what?"

"So, did you like it?"

"Of course I liked it," I said. "Jeez."

"Well I didn't know," she said, bumping her knee against mine. "You didn't say anything."

"Of course I liked it," I said again. I blew a bubble. "And anyway, it's not something you talk about."

"You can if you want," she said.

I put my elbows in the grass and leaned back. I bumped my knee against hers.

"What about you?" I said.

"What about me?"

"Did you like it?" I said.

"Yes."

"Did I do it right?" I asked.

"Yes. You did it perfect."

"I never did it before."

"What, like I have?" she said.

"I don't know," I said. "I thought maybe you had sex books or something. Or went on the Internet."

"To do what?"

"Whatever . . . research," I said.

"Why would I do that?"

"I don't know," I said, grinning at her. She grinned back and looked away down the street.

"No, I didn't do any *research*," she said, quietly. "God, how embarrassing."

We sat for a while, blowing bubbles and listening to the sound of a sprinkler running at the end of the block. She bumped my knee some more. I scooted closer and put my arm around her. She leaned into me and rested her head on my shoulder.

"And now you're a rock star," she said. "Now you're going to be impossible."

★ ★ ★ **28** ★ ★ ★

Kevin had been right. One show with Tiny Masters and I wanted to play more. Unfortunately they only had one more gig scheduled. I called Kevin. He said they hadn't gotten any new gigs because they didn't think I wanted to be in the band. I told him that was ridiculous, of course I wanted to be in the band.

The next week I worked late shifts at Pedro's. I was going to bed at two and three in the morning, which was why I vaguely heard the phone ring very late one night. I fell back asleep then woke up again, with my dad standing in my doorway.

"Hey, Pete," he said. "You awake?"

I lifted my head. "Yeah, what's up?" I said, still dreaming.

"Uncle Joe is sick. I gotta go to Seattle. Uncle Joe is . . . uh . . . he had a heart thing. I gotta go up there."

"What?" I said, not understanding. I lifted my head higher. "What time is it?" It was 4:38 a.m.

"Can you handle yourself here for a couple days?" he said.

"Sure," I said. I was understanding now. I sat up. My father looked like he had not slept. I could smell alcohol from across the room.

"Wait," I said. "Uncle Joe? Where is he?"

"He's in the hospital. In Seattle. Aunt Ruthie just called."

I threw off my covers and swung my legs out of bed.

"You don't need to get up," said my dad.

I got up. I found my bathrobe, the one I never wore. "You're going to drive to Seattle?" I said. "Right now?" My dad got a DUI in Washington State the year before. Another one and they'd throw him in jail.

"I have to," he said. "You'll be okay without a car?"

"Of course," I said. "Are you sure you don't want to sleep first?"

He seemed to think he was okay, but he didn't look good. This whole situation was not good. Uncle Joe and my father were not close. If my dad was being called up there, it must be serious.

"Why don't we eat something?" I said.

My father was too dazed to protest. His hair was sticking out all over. It looked like he might have fallen asleep on the couch, which he often did.

I went to the kitchen. I turned on the light, turned on the stove, quickly threw some butter in a frying pan. That was the best way to make my dad do something. Don't ask. Just do it.

I made eggs and toast. "If he's in the hospital," I said loudly, over the crackling eggs, "that means he's okay. He's stabilized or whatever."

My dad nodded. I slid three fried eggs and toast in front of him. He ate it slowly. I ate too, watching him, trying to figure out if he could drive. It occurred to me I might have to go with him, which I did not want to do. I had to work. Besides, Uncle Joe and Aunt Ruthie were not fun to visit. Uncle Joe was a real estate developer and had already had one heart attack to show for it. He and Aunt Ruthie had lent my dad money. They were probably still lending him money, which Aunt Ruthie was never happy about, and that made for some painful moments the few times we saw them.

Fortunately, my dad got sleepy with the food in him. A glass of orange juice and more toast seemed to finish him off. I convinced him to lie down for a few minutes on the couch. He fell dead asleep. I knew he would. I left him there with a blanket over him. I went back to bed myself. At ten-thirty that morning, he was still there, snoring. At eleven-thirty I woke him up. He showered and dressed and left for Seattle.

At three I called Aunt Ruthie. My dad hadn't arrived. I told her I had made him sleep a few hours, so he might be late.

"I don't know why Joe wants him here," she said. "There's nothing he can do. And I certainly don't need any more people in my house at a time like this."

"I'm sure my dad will leave as soon as he can," I said.

"If he really wanted to help he could stop being such a burden on Joseph," said Aunt Ruthie, her voice breaking suddenly. She started to cry.

"Aunt Ruthie?" I said.

"Relations aren't just for money you know!"

Wow, this must be bad, I thought.

"I'm sorry," she said, sobbing. "But I can't do this again. I can't go through this again."

I told her not to worry, that things would work out. But what did I know? She cried for a while and eventually calmed down. I got off the phone.

★ ★ ★ **29** ★ ★ ★

My dad called the next day. Uncle Joe was okay. They had operated on him that afternoon, and it went smoothly. He would stay in the hospital for a couple of days to make sure everything was okay.

"How's Aunt Ruthie?" I asked.

"She's a basket case," said my dad. "As usual."

"Yeah, she freaked out on the phone."

"Listen, do you need money?" he said. "I'm going to be here for a couple days more."

"Nah, I got everything. I'm fine."

"You sure?"

"There's food. I got my bike. I'm just going to be working anyway."

"When did you become so self-sufficient?" he said, joking.

"I don't know," I said.

"Well, call me here if you need anything."

"Okay. Take care. Say hi to Uncle Joe, or whatever. "

That night, Kevin came over, and we jammed in our basement studio. He had some ideas for songs that we tried to figure out. Later, Jennifer came over and Margaret and Lauren, and we all hung out.

Then Nick called. He had a CD someone burned at the gig we played at Sanctuary; it was recorded directly through the sound system. Of course we all wanted to hear it. We told him to come over.

He showed up with Kim and Chelsea. Kim was Nick's girlfriend, I had learned. She was nice, and she and Jenny and Margaret talked. Chelsea was less friendly. She wanted to know where Billy was. She wouldn't really talk to anyone until he showed up. He did, around eleven. Everybody immediately gathered around the stereo in my living room to listen to the live recording.

It sounded great. I mean, parts of it were too loud and the balance was wrong, but you could hear all the instruments. You could also hear stuff like Nick telling Billy to stop stepping on his cord. Everyone laughed at that. Everyone but Billy. Something was going on with Billy and Chelsea. I guess they were having an argument. Or something. Chelsea was apparently one of those girls who dresses sexy and causes a lot of trouble.

When the recording was over, Billy and Chelsea left. Nick laughed when I asked what was happening between them. He said Chelsea and Billy were in love, in their own "special way." I didn't know what that meant and I was afraid to ask, but I gave Margaret a look like, *See what psychos these people are?*

Kevin suggested we listen to the CD again. Everyone thought that was a great idea. We turned off all the lights and lay on the floor and listened to it really loud. I lay next to Margaret. I closed my eyes and let the music create visions in my mind. The words of "Girl in the Window" made you think of a pretty, flower-lined street. The smooth drum and bass section of "No Man" made you think of a huge barren desert. The hard, pounding intro to "Reckoning" made you think of something big and deadly, coming at you through the woods. The music took you places. It took you out of yourself. Just like *real* bands did.

★★★ 30 ★★★

My dad got back in the middle of the week. I came home from Pedro's, and he was in the basement playing his guitar. He looked tired but pretty good, considering. I plugged in my bass and we jammed on "So What?" Then he played "Midnight Rambler" by the Stones and I joined in on bass and we goofed around on that for a while.

The big news was my second Tiny Masters gig. It was July 29 at a club called Blackbird. It was not an all-ages show, there would be real grown-ups in the audience. We were playing with two bands, Separate Chex and The Lab. The Lab were two guys who did everything with keyboards and computers. They were big in Portland. That's what Nick said.

That night Kim and Chelsea showed up and hung out in the parking lot before we played. Kim and Chelsea were both dressed really hot. It was weird because they were only sixteen. I don't know where they got miniskirts and fishnets and all that. Also, from the moment she arrived, Chelsea was looking for trouble. You could see it in her face. She went straight to Billy and accused him of something. I didn't hear what. They walked around to the side of the club to talk in private. When they came back they were fighting even worse. Chelsea marched angrily toward the street with Billy following. "Chelsea! Chelsea, would you wait a second!" he said. She wouldn't turn around. Nick told Billy to come back, we were about to go onstage. Billy followed her into the street. "Would you listen to me for one second! Chelsea! *Chelsea!!*" She ran through the traffic; people honked and swerved to avoid her. "I swear to God—!" threatened Billy, kicking gravel into the traffic. Chelsea flipped him off from the opposite side of the street. Billy picked up a rock, hesitated . . . and threw it into the ground.

"Let her go, Billy," said Nick. "We gotta play."

"That Chelsea," Kevin whispered to me. "She knows how to stir things up."

+++

Fifteen minutes later we started our set. There were a lot of people, but they had never heard of us, so they just stared, waiting for us to prove ourselves.

Boy, did we *not* prove ourselves. On the first song, Billy got confused and played the chorus before he was supposed to. Nick tried to sing, but Billy kept playing over him. Kevin tried to pull us together, but Billy wasn't paying attention. The song literally fell apart. Nick waved for us to stop. I couldn't believe it. Didn't he know that you never do that? It was the first rule of playing out. It was the first thing my dad ever taught me: no matter how bad you mess up, *you never stop.*

★★★ **31** ★★★

We stopped. The crowd stared at us. I exchanged helpless looks with Kevin. Nick glared at Billy. "*What are you doing?*" he hissed at his brother.

Billy said nothing, but the fury in his face answered the question. Billy was still thinking about Chelsea. In his mind, he was still back in the parking lot screaming at her across the street.

Nick tried to talk to him. Billy turned his back. He went to his amp and strummed a chord. It sounded terrible; he was completely out of tune. I tried to give him a low E, but he ignored it. "Billy," I said, under my breath, "*Tune up!*" He looked at me with utter contempt. "*You guys!*" hissed Kevin. We were now breaking the second rule of playing live: *Never argue in front of an audience.*

Billy suddenly launched into the next song. No one was ready, which didn't matter, since he started it with a furious blast of power chords. That was not how the song was supposed to start. He kept bashing away, playing something I had never heard before. Kevin, baffled, started drumming. Nick joined in. I did too. Eventually it started to sound like the song we were supposed to be playing. But then Billy went totally crazy. He tore into a feedback guitar solo right in the middle of the chorus. I was dumbstruck. *What on earth was he doing?* I turned to Kevin, to indicate this was the final straw, but Kevin was going with it. He had that excited shine in his eyes. It was like he had been waiting for this all along. I saw Nick was doing the same thing. They were locking onto Billy's craziness, and they were going to drive it as hard and fast as they possibly could.

So that's what I did. I had no choice. I played the simplest bass line I could think of, anchoring the noise and the distortion and the feedback. The whole situation was so reckless and insane it was actually scary. I had actual goose bumps going up my back and over my arms. And it kept building. It sounded like a tank crashing through a house, through a series of houses. Kevin was pounding like I'd never seen him. Nick was rocking back and forth. I was playing so hard my hand was cramping. But where were we going? How was this going to end?

Then Billy's guitar fell off. His strap must have broken. His guitar bounced off the monitor and landed at his feet. He stared at it for a moment. Then he kicked it across the floor. Then he ran to it, picked it up, and threw it across the stage at his amplifier, where it knocked over a pitcher of water and just missed a girl who had crawled onto the stage to see better.

Kevin and I kept playing, but the song soon collapsed into a confused, noisy mess. That's when I remembered the audience. I had completely forgotten they were there. Now I looked. The people were stunned. They were in shock.

Then they exploded into applause.

★★★ **32** ★★★

Two days later Kevin came into Pedro's. The lunch rush had just passed and I was clearing tables. Kevin sauntered in and followed me to the kitchen. "Nice apron," he said.

"Thanks," I said.

He tossed a copy of the *Portland Edge* on the counter. "Have you seen the review?"

"What review?"

"Dude, the review in that paper."

I looked at the *Portland Edge*.

"Page fifty-six."

I picked it up. I opened it to page fifty-six. It was a local music column. "The Lab Reveal Their Clinical Side" was the headline. The article read:

> Blackbird patrons gathered eagerly last weekend to see The Lab, local electro-pop favorites who are said to be close to signing with Capital Records. The success must be going to their heads, as their cold, emotionless set fell flat Saturday night. It did not help their cause that newcomers The Tiny Masters of Today

preceded them. These youngsters delivered a raucous set of crude power rock that teetered between sublime rapture and total anarchy. Disaster seemed to wait at every turn for the Tiny Masters, but a driving bass and drum combination never lost its footing and pounded the stunned crowd into submission.

The column continued, talking more about The Lab and their record deal. I skimmed it to the bottom. I went back to the top and read about us again.

When I'd finished, I put the paper down.

Kevin nodded his head at me. A wide grin was spread across his face. "You read the part about the bass and drum?" he said.

"Yeah," I said.

"Dude, that's us! That's you and me. We kicked ass!"

"Yeah, I guess we did." I picked up the paper and started through the column a third time.

"We can't let it go to our heads though," cautioned Kevin. "We gotta be chill. We can't even say anything. I mean, except to our girlfriends."

"What did Billy and Nick say?"

"They were like, *whatever*. They expect it."

"They do?"

"Of course. They think they're going to be famous. They've always thought that."

"Famous?" I said. "They're *lucky* is more like it. That gig was a joke. If any other critic—"

"Hey, what do we care? Maybe this guy's right. Maybe we're geniuses teetering between anarchy and total whatever. But we still rocked it, right?"

"Yeah," I said.

"Dude, give me high five!"

I gave him high five.

"I gotta call Jenny. She'll be stoked. You guys got a phone here?"

★ ★ ★ 33 ★ ★ ★

I couldn't wait to show my dad the review. I went home and defrosted some lasagna, which was one of his favorites. I put the *Portland Edge* out, where he would see it first thing. He didn't come home though. I got out my bass and practiced Tiny Masters songs in front of the TV until ten. Finally I heard his car come in the driveway. I put my bass away. I ran to the door to meet him. Then I thought better of it and went back to the couch. I tried to act casual.

He came in. His eyes were red. He had a smoky, perfumed smell about him.

"Hey, Dad," I called from the couch.

"Hey," he said.

I couldn't resist. I got up and grabbed the *Portland Edge*. "Check this out," I said as he lowered his shoulder bag. I jammed the paper into his hands.

"What is it?" he said.

"It's a review. Of Tiny Masters."

He took the paper to the kitchen table. "Can I fix a drink first?"

I knew he was going to do this. I had to wait. "Do you want me to read it to you?" I said.

"No, no, I'll read it." He made his drink. He sat down. He opened the paper to page fifty-six and read the column. I watched his face as he did. He looked studious at first. He raised an eyebrow. He smiled. Then he sat back, his eyes still on the paper. "Wow, good for you. Sounds like quite a show."

"Isn't that amazing?" I crowed. "And the best part. The drum and bass . . . pounded the crowd. . . ." I pointed it out to him. "That's me and Kevin!"

"It sure is," he said, scanning the article again. "You don't mind being called *crude*?"

"It is kind of how we sound," I said, sitting down across from him. "The thing is . . . like that night, Billy was freaking out about his girlfriend. And he kind of went ballistic. Right onstage. He was banging his guitar, and doing feedback, and just ripping into these crazy solos."

"Sounds pretty . . . chaotic."

"No but it's like a painting that's got paint thrown all over. It was this noisy mess he makes . . . that *we* make."

"Sounds too crazy for me," said my dad, getting that look he sometimes gets when he doesn't understand the trends of the moment.

"But it was intense," I said. "That was the thing. And during one song, Billy's guitar fell off. Because he was hitting it so hard. And while it was lying there, he kicked it! Like across the stage. The people were like—"

My dad frowned. I remembered suddenly how much he hated people who abused their instruments. We had once seen that Nirvana video where Kurt Cobain rams his guitar through his speaker, and my dad got furious. He considered it the worst offense a musician could commit.

"I mean," I said quickly, "he didn't *break it* or anything. He wasn't trying to hurt it, but since it fell off and was lying there at his feet . . . you know his strap got tangled around his foot. Everyone thought it was cool. I mean, that wasn't the important part. . . ."

My dad frowned more. He drank his drink and looked into the kitchen. "Is that the frozen lasagna?" he said.

★★★ 34 ★★★

Of course I had called Margaret from Pedro's, to tell her about the review. She was at the mall and promptly ran off to find a copy of the *Portland Edge*.

I called her now, from my room.

"Did you show your dad?" she asked. She had a knack for finding your sore spot instantly.

"Yeah, I showed him," I said, softly.

"What? Didn't he like it?"

"Yeah, he liked it. I screwed up though. I told him about Billy kicking his guitar."

"What about it?"

"Dad doesn't like people who smash their instruments."

"Well. It was just one thing that happened. And it wasn't in the review."

"I know. He liked the review. I guess he did. He thinks it sounds weird. He doesn't understand some things I guess."

"Like what doesn't he understand?"

"You know, that something that extreme can still be music."

"I thought you said he was in metal bands, and wore spandex pants? That's pretty extreme."

"Yeah, but to him that's still real music."

"Well, whatever. He's your dad anyway. He's not supposed to be your biggest fan. He's supposed to be your dad."

I didn't say anything back. "What are you doing?" I said.

"Nothing, lying here on my bed."

"Me too," I said. I scratched my stomach with a guitar pick.

"Peter?" said Margaret.

"Yeah?"

"Do you ever think about your mom?"

"Sometimes."

"Because you never say anything about her."

"I don't?"

"No. Nothing. It's kind of odd."

"I think about her."

"I mean, if it's too uncomfortable."

"It's not too uncomfortable."

"It just seems like . . . like sometimes I want to ask you about her. Or say something. But I'm afraid to."

"Like what?" I said.

"Like what would she think of the review, or something like that."

"She would probably think it was weird."

"Or that time we went to the mall and I helped you buy those shoes. That's something a mom would do."

"I don't need help buying my clothes."

"No, but I'm just saying—"

"She was a folksinger anyway, I don't think she went to the mall very much. She wasn't very materialistic."

94

There was a long silence. "Do you think I'm too material-istic?" she asked.

"No, no, I just mean . . . I'd probably have to buy my own shoes anyway."

"Yeah."

"We have pictures of her," I said. "If you want to see sometime."

"But do you remember her? In your own memory?"

"Not really."

"But you were seven when she died. You must remember something."

"She had black hair," I said.

"That's all?"

"And she was . . . tall I guess. As tall as my dad. He told me that once."

"What else does he say about her?"

"Not much," I said. "I mean, she was a great musician. But so is my dad."

"It must be hard for him."

"We're used to it," I said. "He has girlfriends and stuff. He's moved on."

"But what about you?"

"And me too. You have to deal with it. You have to keep going."

"I guess," she said.

"I mean if you want to see the pictures sometime . . ."

"No, not if you don't want to."

"I want to, I just . . . I can't think about it too much. You know? You can't spend your life thinking about things you don't have."

★★★ **35** ★★★

After the second Tiny Masters gig, summer slowed down. The Carlisle brothers went out of town, Kevin was with Jenny most of the time, I would work and go to Lauren's after.

Travis and Lauren were finally hanging out. Travis would cruise by in his car. He said he only wanted to be friends, but you could tell he liked all the attention Lauren gave him. Margaret said he would fool around with her sometimes, and afterward claim they were just friends. Margaret didn't approve of it, but there wasn't much she could do.

Sometimes Brian came with Travis. I never saw his girl-friend. He made me nervous. Sometimes when they were both at Lauren's it seemed like the four of them—since they worked at the mall—were better friends and I was the odd man out, like they knew all the gossip about people and all the soap operas.

One night they came over and Brian had just turned seventeen. To celebrate, the five of us drove to the Willamette River to go night swimming. When we got there everyone took off their clothes and jumped in. I wasn't expecting the *taking off our clothes* part, but I did it.

Lauren was all over Travis in the water. They were laughing and dunking each other. They swam downriver and disappeared into the next cove. That left Margaret and Brian and me. Brian was being cool and acting like he would leave us alone if we wanted but Margaret didn't want him feeling left out. So the three of us swam around, naked. We talked, or tried to, while we huffed and puffed from treading water against the current. Brian seemed very cool and very confident. When he and Margaret talked it was like their voices went down into this special whisper. Like they knew each other in this special way. It was hard for me, it was hard in general, in the cold water, naked, in the dark.

In mid-August, my dad drove to Seattle to see my Uncle Joe again. Aunt Ruthie called me that same week and apologized for freaking out on the phone. She asked me about my music, since that's all she knew about me. I told her I was in the jazz band at school. It was too hard to explain Tiny Masters to adults.

My dad was gone for several days, and I had the place to myself. One night after Pedro's I got bored and decided to find some pictures of my mom for Margaret. There was one big cardboard box that had most of our family mementos in it. It was in my dad's closet, stuck behind some other stuff. I pulled it into the middle of the room and dug through it.

It wasn't organized very well. It wasn't really organized at all. The photographs were loose and floating around. There were old letters, some in envelopes, some not. There were old concert ticket stubs, my dad's old passport, some old fliers from my dad's first band. It kind of made me mad he left it all scattered like that. But I wasn't going to clean it up.

I gathered all the pictures I could find with my mother in them. I kneeled on the floor to look at them. I'd seen them all before. My favorites were a series of her playing an acoustic guitar. Her hair was long and black and she wore a white lace shirt. It was kind of shocking how beautiful she was. I wondered what Margaret would think. Would your girlfriend be jealous of your mom? Or was it a bonding thing, like they wanted to be *like* your mom?

I put those pictures in a stack and looked for more. I dug through the box. Then a cassette appeared at the bottom. I was surprised to see it. It was the famous "black cassette." I had looked through this box many times in recent years and had never come across it. I had wondered if it still existed, or if my dad had put it somewhere else.

The famous "black cassette" was a tape my dad recorded of my mother the night he first met her. It was a crude tape, recorded on the Walkman my dad had in his pocket the night he stumbled into the café where she was playing. It was famous because when I was nine, he had sat me down in the living room, explained to me what it was, and played it for me. At the sound of my mother's voice I had burst into tears. I had nightmares for weeks.

My father felt terrible, and we never listened to it again. I had assumed he had locked it away somewhere I would never find it. But no, here it was.

I lifted it out of the box. I studied it. It was a Memorex Ultra 90. On the faded label was written: "Metro Café, Seattle, 3/85." I tried turning the spools with my finger, to see if they still worked. They did.

I looked at the tape itself. The thin brown strip looked fine. It looked like it would play. I took it into the living room and put it in our main stereo. I made sure it was positioned correctly. Old tapes could get eaten if you weren't careful.

I pushed play. I listened. The tape began to hiss. A snatch

of another song came on, probably the thing my dad taped over. There was a few seconds of silence, a loud click, and then you could hear it: the jostling sounds of a small crowded room. This was it. This was the Metro Café in March of 1985. I put my finger on Stop, in case I needed to turn it off.

There was a strum and my mother said thank you and people clapped. You could hear talking and someone ordering something from a waitress. My father must have started recording in the middle of the set. My mother said something else, away from the microphone. I couldn't hear and I turned up the volume until the hiss of the old Memorex filled the living room.

My mother began to play a soft arpeggio on her guitar. The audience immediately quieted, and my mother began to sing. Her voice was beautiful in a strange ethereal way. I had heard other recordings of my mother, clear studio recordings of her later work. This was different. There was something unguarded and unprotected about this. All of her was there. It made me close my eyes and bow my head.

But I kept listening. I let it play. The lyrics were about a boy who doesn't know himself, and a girl who falls in love with him. The chorus was:

Into the heart
Into a sea of love
She will wait for him
She will stay for him

The audience loved it. When she finished they clapped and whistled. There was more background noise. My dad said something. I rewound, turned up the volume, and played it again. You could hear my dad talking to someone. He said, "I know, I know, but who is she?"

The next song started. I listened. It was faster; it sounded like an old folk song. The sound quality was especially bad on that one, but people were into it. They all clapped in unison at one point. Afterward people were laughing and talking and you could tell everyone loved my mom. She was having a great gig.

The third song was slow again. The melody was higher but my mom sang the notes easily, gracefully. The chorus had a cool hitch in it, an odd beat-hesitation, the mark of some-one who knew what they were doing. And she was such a good guitar player. I had never really listened to that before.

Then the tape ended. It just stopped in the middle of the song. That was it. Two and a half songs. I watched the tape spin silently in the cassette deck. I wanted more now. But that was all there was.

Downtime

★★★ **36** ★★★

At the end of August there was a mini-heat wave. It was a hundred degrees every day. Pedro's got really busy, since it was too hot to cook. The waiters and I made some of our best money.

My dad came back from Seattle. I didn't talk to him much about his trip. Uncle Joe was recovering, Aunt Ruthie was a mess, there wasn't much else to say.

Margaret and her parents had gone to Idaho for two weeks to visit her grandparents. That was not easy. Her parents didn't want us talking on the phone during the vacation for some reason. Her mom had always been paranoid about the two of us. Maybe she found out we were having sex.

Before Margaret left I thought I would be okay with it. I thought it might be good being by myself for a while. I was wrong. It was agony. From the moment she left I was totally lost. I lay in bed at night with my phone in my hands and no one to call. During the day I rode my bike to work, breathing in the dust and car exhaust and feeling like I was the last person on earth. When had I become so dependent? Without her I didn't know what to do with myself.

Kevin tried to cheer me up. He took me to a party at the house where the All Girl Summer Fun Band lived. There were lots of music people, lots of college people. Two girls who had seen us at Blackbird came up to us and wanted to know about Tiny Masters and when we were playing again. "You guys rock!" said another guy.

Nick and Billy showed up. They were being very cool and hanging out in the living room, where the other musicians were. Kevin and I went to the backyard to get some beer, but they were out of plastic cups so Kevin went to find some.

That's when I spotted Chelsea. She was standing by herself in the grass. She was talking on her cell phone. She saw me, looked away, then turned and looked at me again. She waved for me to come over.

I pointed at myself. She had never spoken to me, or acknowledged me in any way. What could she want?

She waved again, more emphatically than before.

I walked toward her, carefully, trying to act casual or whatever. I was afraid of Chelsea.

She was listening intently to her cell phone. Her purse was swinging on her elbow. She had a plastic cup of keg beer.

"Here," she told me. "Hold this." She handed me the beer. I took it. It was some sort of microbrew. I lifted the cup to smell it.

"Don't drink it! Gross!"

"Oh," I said. "Sorry."

I held the beer at waist level. Chelsea redialed her phone. She flipped her hair away from her ear and listened for an answer.

I stood and waited. Chelsea turned away from me to hear better. She wasn't getting through. She redialed again and listened again. I'd never been this close to her before. She was even prettier close up. Her perfect skin, her hair, the brightness of her blue eyes. She was like a queen. It was intoxicating.

When no one answered, she slapped her cell phone shut. She threw it in her purse.

"So what's your name again?" she said, taking back her cup.

"Pete. Or Peter. Sometimes people—"

"Do you have twenty dollars?"

"Uh . . ." I said. I instinctively patted my wallet. I pulled it from my back pocket. I had seventeen dollars.

"Actually, do you have forty dollars?" said Chelsea.

"I don't," I said.

"Well, do you think you could get it?"

"How would I get it?" I said.

She looked at me like I was stupid. "Like ask one of your friends?"

"I don't think anyone has it."

"How much money do you have?"

"Seventeen dollars," I said. "But I kind of need it."

"Jesus," said Chelsea, rolling her eyes. "Well, can you at least walk me to the cash machine?"

★★★ **37** ★★★

According to Chelsea there was a cash machine down the street at the Gas and Food Mart. She complained as we walked because she didn't have her car. She complained about her friend Francesca who was supposed to meet her at the party. She complained about the charges on cash machines, though she quickly explained it wasn't her money anyway, it was her mom's ATM card.

We got to the Gas and Food Mart. Chelsea went to the cash machine and I got a Slurpee. When Chelsea saw it she wanted one too. She asked me to make her one and left me to pay for it, which I did, not knowing what else to do.

Outside, Chelsea was making another call. I held her Slurpee while she dialed.

"What do you need the twenty dollars for?" I asked.

She looked at me like I was retarded. She held the phone to her ear.

I wished Margaret were back. Not that it wasn't fun standing outside the Gas and Food Mart being abused by beautiful Chelsea. That was fun too, but it would be better if Margaret was around to see it.

No one answered for Chelsea. "You're not going to be in Tiny Masters anymore," said Chelsea casually. She dialed a new number. "Billy's friend Jason is coming back from California."

"What?" I said.

"They're kicking you out," she said. She put her finger in her ear to drown me out if anyone answered.

"Who told you that?" I said.

She didn't answer.

"They're not kicking me out," I said.

"Yes, they are."

"Yeah?" I said. "When?"

"As soon as Jason gets back from California."

"They didn't say anything to me about it."

She shrugged. "It's Billy. What do you expect? He'll screw anyone over."

"But I already played two gigs with them."

"So what," she said. "Jason's their friend. And he's way cooler than you. He dyes his hair. He has tattoos."

"Yeah, but he can't play," I said. "I heard the rehearsal CD."

Chelsea shrugged. Someone answered her call. She turned away from me. "Francesca!" she said. "Where are you? . . . No, I was at the Summer Fun Girl party . . . It's okay . . . right now? I'm standing outside a gas station with some guy . . . What are you guys doing? . . . Can you pick me up, I'm kind of car-less at the moment. . . ."

★ ★ ★ **38** ★ ★ ★

I left. I put Chelsea's Slurpee on the curb and walked back toward the party. Chelsea might have said something to me, asked me where I was going, but I didn't answer.

I walked down the dark street. I thought about Margaret.

I didn't talk to her in my head like I normally did. I just saw her. I thought about what she looked like and imagined her in various places, sitting at the bus stop or standing behind the counter at Nature First.

Back at the house, the party was going strong. I walked up the steps and went in the front door. Billy was standing with some other musicians in the living room. I came up behind him and shoved him. He knocked into the guy he was talking to. They both turned to see who it was. I shoved Billy again. He tripped over the coffee table and almost fell. "What the—?" he said. I shoved him a third time, and this time he shoved back. I swung at him, he swung at me, and all hell broke loose. We grabbed each other, pushed each other, stumbled backward over the coffee table, and fell over the couch. I ripped his shirt half off. He punched me in the mouth. Then Kevin yanked me backward. Nick grabbed me too; everyone in the room jumped in to pull us apart. Billy was crazed by now and wanted to fight more. He tried to tear loose from the people holding him. He snarled at me. He said he'd kill me. He swore and spit. He said he'd rip my head off.

I didn't care. I wasn't afraid of him. I stared back. I stood there and watched him and stared right back.

An hour later Kevin and I were in his car, outside my house. I had the bottom of my T-shirt in my hand, I was using it to dab my bleeding lip.

Kevin hadn't said a word. Now he spoke. "Can I just say one thing?"

I didn't answer.

"What . . . on earth . . . *were you thinking?*"

I stared straight ahead. "They're kicking me out of the band," I said quietly. "What difference does it make?"

Kevin stared out his window. "How do you know they're kicking you out?" he said.

"Chelsea told me."

He nodded. He thought about that. "And you believed her?"

"Why wouldn't I?" I said. "They don't like me. They've never liked me."

"They don't like *anybody*. They want to be famous. That's all they care about."

I dabbed at my lip. "Did you know?" I asked.

Kevin sighed. "I could tell they were thinking about it."

"You weren't going to stick up for me?"

"Of course I was going to stick up for you," he said. "Don't be an idiot. Do you think I want to play with that other guy? But there were other ways to handle it. There were other things to consider."

"Like what?"

"Like *timing*."

"How long were you going to wait?"

"Dude, the situation would have fixed itself. That other guy sucks. They would have seen it themselves. . . ."

I stared out my window.

"Instead," said Kevin, "you do this. Now what do we do? Now we have no chance."

★ ★ ★ **39** ★ ★ ★

The next day was Friday. My dad went to work. I slept in. I called Margaret, who was supposed to get back that weekend. She had to, school started on Monday. But no one was home. I listened to her mother's voice say, "This is the Little residence, we can't take your call right now. . . ." I left a message after the beep.

On Saturday I rode my bike by her house. They weren't home yet. The house was empty and quiet like it had been. That night there was still no answer when I called.

On Sunday I called all day. I called twice in the afternoon, three times in the evening. Suddenly, at ten-fifteen someone answered.

"Hello," said her dad.

"Hello? Mr. Little? It's Peter."

"Oh. Hello, Peter."

"Is Margaret there?"

"She's busy at the moment."

"Can she come to the phone?"

"Not at the moment."

That was odd. "Are you guys back from vacation?"

"Yes, Peter, we are."

"Can she call me back?"

"I don't think so," he said.

I swallowed.

"It's after ten," he said. "I think that's too late to be making social calls."

"Oh," I said. "Sorry."

"We've driven all day, and everyone is tired. She's going to bed as soon as she's unpacked."

Mr. Little had always been nice to me. This was not like him. Something was going on.

"She'll be at school tomorrow," he said. "I suggest you speak with her then."

At Evergreen the next morning everyone was in back-to-school mode: running around, greeting people, reconnecting with old friends. I stood at my locker, scanning the packed hallway, trying to figure out where Margaret was.

Robert Hatch appeared. "Hey," he said. "Wudup?"

"Hey," I said. I couldn't quite face him for some reason. I looked at my books.

"What's the matter?" he said.

"Nothing, how was summer camp?"

"It was great. I hung out with a girl."

"Really?" I said.

"I'll tell you about it at lunch. What's the matter with you? Where's Margaret. You guys are still . . . ?"

I nodded that we were. "I haven't seen her though. She's been on vacation."

"Everything still cool?"

I tried to nod, but it turned into something else.

"You look different," he said.

"Do I?"

"Yeah," he said, studying me for a moment. "I'll see you at lunch. Her name is Elise, by the way, the girl I met. She lives in Seattle. She's a senior though. She's an *older woman*."

"An older woman," I said.

I finally found Margaret's locker fourth period, just before lunch. She was at the opposite end of the junior/senior wing, as far away as you could get. "Margaret!" I called to her. Lauren was there too, but she left as I approached.

"Margaret, what's up?" I said.

"Hey, Pete."

I wanted to hug her but I couldn't in the hall.

"Your dad seemed mad about something," I said. "I called last night."

"I know," said Margaret. She was avoiding looking at me.

"What is it? What's going on?"

"They found out," she said, quietly. She glanced up and down the hall. "They know we've been having sex."

"How did they find out?"

"They just . . ." she said. "My mom found out."

"Did you tell her?"

"I didn't mean to." She struggled to get a textbook out of her backpack. "It was an accident. I didn't know it would be such a shock."

"Why did you tell her?"

She frowned. She shook her head. "I just did, okay? I thought it would be all right. . . ." She looked tired and disgusted. I wanted to touch her, to comfort her, but I couldn't, not in the hall.

I jammed my hands in my back pockets. "Did you tell them we love each other?"

"They don't care about that," she said with quiet force. "They think I'm bad now. They're acting like I did something terrible, something to them."

"That's ridiculous."

"I don't know what their problem is. They're just being impossible. My dad was like . . . he wouldn't talk to me. . . ."

"But your dad has always been so cool."

"Not about this," she said.

I shook my head. I looked around at the other students. They seemed happy, content, oblivious.

"They fought the whole vacation," said Margaret. "My mom was blaming my dad and my dad was blaming my mom. And my stupid grandparents . . ." Margaret looked into her locker. "My dad might call your dad."

"Oh great," I said.

Margaret shut her locker. "Another thing, I have to hang out with Lauren at lunch."

"Why?"

"Travis dumped her. She's very upset. She's not eating."

"But I haven't seen you in two weeks!"

"I'm sorry, Peter, I can't help it. Things are just bad right now."

I stared at her. She walked by me and down the hall.

★★★ **40** ★★★

"At first Elise seemed sort of stuck up," said Robert Hatch. We were at McDonald's after school. Margaret had gone somewhere with Lauren. "Like I'd see her at the tennis courts and she'd be like, she wouldn't even say hi or anything. And she was blonde and pretty and I was thinking I had no chance. And this other counselor sort of liked her too but he went for the girl who did canoeing so that sort of cleared the way for me."

I stirred my milk shake with my straw. Robert ate some of my fries. "So what happened?" I said.

"So what happened was, after about two weeks, she came over to me during a campfire and started talking. So I was like, why don't we go for a walk?"

I nodded. I looked out the window.

"So that's when we first made out. Can you believe it? And she gave me this anklet. . . ." He lifted his foot so I could see a dirty band woven around his ankle. "So we're going to e-mail and talk on the phone. Maybe I can go up there at Christmas, or she can come visit. You can get Amtrak for seventy-nine dollars. I'm already jealous though. Guys really like her. Do you ever get jealous of Margaret?"

I hadn't heard anything past the "anklet." "Margaret?" I said.

"What's up with you? You're barely listening to me."

"No, I am," I said. "Of course I am. That's great. She sounds cool."

"I know you and Margaret have done a lot more, but for me this is sort of big."

"I didn't say it wasn't."

"What's going on with her?" he asked. "Where is she?"

"She's with Lauren. That guy Travis dumped her."

"Wait? Lauren had a boyfriend?"

"Sort of, it was that mall guy."

"She's anorexic, right?"

"I don't know. Margaret said she just has a high metabolism. She has to eat milk shakes and stuff."

"Jeez, I'd take Lauren out for a milk shake," said Robert.

"Yeah?" I said.

"I mean, not now, since I have a girlfriend. But I would have."

That night my dad was home when I came in. He was trying to make dinner. Generally when we had a sit-down dinner I made it. I was a better cook, I was usually home earlier, it had become our habit.

But I hadn't been around. All that weekend I'd been eating at Pedro's. And when I was home I'd kept to myself. So I wasn't surprised to see him there, with bread and eggs, volunteering to make French toast. The fact was, I'd been avoiding him, and he knew it.

He made dinner and we sat down and ate. I had so much on my mind. I hadn't told him about the fight with Billy. I hadn't told him about Margaret and her parents. I hadn't said anything about the Metro Café tape. It was like I couldn't let the dam break, like if I said one thing, then I'd have to say all of it, and then I'd end up crying or something ridiculous.

I didn't look at him. I spread butter on my French toast.

"How was your first day of school?" he asked.

"All right," I said.

"I can't believe you're a junior already," he said, shaking his head.

I nodded. I poured syrup.

"What classes are you taking?" he said. "If you don't mind my asking."

I shrugged. "Spanish. Math. The usual." I cut a corner off my French toast and jammed it into my mouth.

"That's funny you do so well at Spanish. I couldn't do languages to save my life."

I didn't answer.

He ate. I ate. The doorbell rang.

The doorbell at our house didn't ring very often. We lived on a tiny street between Highway 26 and Canyon Road that was hard to get to. It was not a location you would be passing by.

I got up. I wiped my sticky hands with a paper towel. I went to the door. It was Eric Simon. I hadn't seen him since our last Mad Skillz gig in June.

"Peter, hey," he said. "What's up, man?"

"Hey, Eric."

He waved through the door to my dad. "Hey, Mr. McGrady."

"Hi, Eric," my dad called back.

Eric smiled at me. "I was just in the neighborhood.

Wanted to see how school was. I was getting nostalgic. Now that I don't have to go there anymore."

"Oh," I said. I couldn't tell if he was joking.

"No, but seriously," he said. "I wanted to talk to you about Mad Skillz. You know, touch base. You got a second? You wanna go for a drive?"

I gestured behind me, that I was in the middle of dinner. But I thought again. "Yeah, actually," I said. "I'll go for a drive."

I yelled to my dad that I'd be back later. I got into Eric's car.

"Todd's out man, I can't deal with that guy anymore," Eric told me as he steered us onto Highway 26. He wore sunglasses. Some New Age funk thing played on the stereo. "You should have seen the crap he was pulling over the summer. He wanted his share of the money out of the band fund. You know, like what's in the band fund, like a hundred bucks? And it's for the band. That's why it's called the band fund."

"Yeah, he seemed kind of pissed off," I said.

"He needs to get a job. He just hangs out in his parents' basement, watching TV."

"That's not good," I said.

"I hooked up with this other guy. Jeff Weiland. He's a music teacher at the community college. He does a lot of work with keyboards and computers. He says we can record stuff and play it back while we're performing. Backing tracks."

"Huh," I said.

"You gotta meet this guy. He has some good ideas about the set list and about like, moving away from the rock thing a little."

"Into what?" I said.

"More eclectic stuff. Reggae, Caribbean, stuff like that."

"You can't play Caribbean at an eighth-grade dance," I said.

"No, of course not. You stay with the Top Forty when you need to. You just integrate. There's this World Music Festival we can enter up in Port Townsend. First prize is a recording contract with that new Windermere label in Seattle."

I was having trouble grasping this. "So you want to have a band that's half reggae, half rock, and plays eighth-grade dances?"

"Why not?" said Eric. "We have the technology. Why limit yourself?"

"How old is Jeff?"

"He's older. He's a music teacher. He's like thirty, but he likes playing with young people. I already told him about you and your dad and all that."

When Eric was done selling me on the new Mad Skillz, I had him drop me off on Lauren's street. I walked to her house and rang the bell. Her mom came to the door, and her dad. That seemed unnecessary. Or did everybody's parents think I was evil now? Lauren finally came to the door. She made everyone leave and she came outside and shut the door. We walked down her driveway.

"So what's going on with Margaret?" I asked when we seemed far enough from the house.

"It's bad," she said.

"What's bad?"

"Margaret's dad called her a slut," she said, quietly.

"He did *what*!?" I said. "That's ridiculous. What's he thinking? A lot of people—"

"Shhh—" she said.

"But that's such crap—"

"I know," she said. "But Margaret never fights with her parents. Their whole family is freaking out."

"I can't believe he would say that."

"It was in the heat of an argument. Apparently it ruined their vacation."

I shook my head. I stared down the street. "So what should I do?"

"I don't know. Nothing probably."

"Should I go over there?"

"It's not just about you. She's not doing as good in school. Last semester was the first time she didn't get straight As."

"*Straight As*? Who gives a—?"

"But that's the thing. *They* do. And Margaret's standing up to them. She's never fought back before. And she's the oldest. They can't handle it."

"I should go over there."

"No. That would make it worse. You should just stay away for a while."

"I've been away for two weeks! I can barely stand it. Can you call her? Can she come over here?"

"My mom is friends with her mom." She looked back toward her house. We were probably being watched.

"Christ," I said. "This is unbelievable."

119

"Well, at least she still loves you. Travis dumped me on my ass."

"Yeah, I heard," I said. I looked down the street again.

"He just started hanging out with this other girl," she said. "He wouldn't even tell me. The girl's *friend* had to tell me. And she was like, *if you can't satisfy your man*. What the hell does that mean?"

"Travis isn't a man," I said.

"I know, but I still liked him," she said. She blinked like she might start crying. She pulled out a crumpled tissue she had in her pocket.

"I'm sorry," I said. I watched her dab her face. She had pretty eyes. She was pretty in general. But she was so skinny. Her elbows and arms looked like sticks.

★ ★ ★ **42** ★ ★ ★

At school I met Margaret at her locker. "We gotta talk," I said. "Like *today*."

"I know."

"When?" I said.

"After school."

I walked away.

I ate lunch with Kevin and some of his senior friends. I asked Kevin if he had played with Tiny Master again. He hadn't.

"Did Billy say anything about the fight?"

"No, but Nick was telling me about Jason. He gets back next week. I guess he's the new bass player."

"Figures," I said.

"How's Margaret?"

"Terrible. Her parents found out we had sex," I said.

"Ouch."

"I know. It's causing serious problems," I said.

"That's a tough one," said Kevin. At that moment, Sarah Vandeway and Allison Greely walked by. The senior table went quiet as they passed.

"I don't know what to do about it," I told Kevin.

"Parents get weird about sex stuff. I don't know why. It's not like they didn't do it."

Meanwhile, Robert Hatch was mad at me. I sat with him and some other guys in study hall, but Robert was barely acknowledging me. He was still telling everyone who would listen about his new girlfriend. Maybe he didn't want me around because I had a real girlfriend.

Or I used to have one.

Margaret and I met on the front lawn after school. We walked toward her house. She didn't talk. I didn't talk. It was okay though. It was such a relief to be near her, I was at least happy for that.

"Robert Hatch got a girlfriend at summer camp," I said finally.

"He did?"

"Isn't that weird?"

"No, he could have a girlfriend. He's cute."

We walked.

"So are your parents calming down?" I said.

"Not yet. A little, I guess."

"How's Lauren doing?"

"She's okay, she said you were nice to her when you went to her house."

I walked. "So this thing with your parents, it isn't going to change us, is it?"

She hesitated. "I don't know," she said.

I wasn't expecting that. My knees suddenly felt like they couldn't quite hold my weight. I swallowed. "I still love you, you know," I said.

"I know," she said.

We got to the Handy Mart by her house. She didn't want me to come any farther. We sat on the curb, on the side, behind the ice machine. I picked up twigs and threw them into the woods.

Margaret stared into the trees.

"You know, we don't have to have sex," I said. "If that will help."

There was a little bird standing on the edge of the asphalt.

"I wasn't thinking of that as an option," she said.

"Well, it is one."

"It doesn't really matter, the damage is done. We can't go back now."

I picked up a bigger stick and rubbed it against the cement curb. I sharpened it. "There's all these things I need to tell you," I said.

"Like what?"

"I got kicked out of Tiny Masters."

"You did? Oh my God. When?"

"Last week. I got in a fight with Billy."

"An actual fight?"

I nodded. I concentrated on my stick. I could feel Margaret watching me.

"And Eric wants me back in Mad Skillz," I said. "It sounds so dumb compared to Tiny Masters. And I know how much you like Tiny Masters and all those people."

"I would love you no matter what," she said quietly. "I don't care which band you're in."

"Why are you doing this then?"

"Doing what?"

"Acting like you might . . . break up with me." Something stuck in my throat when I said it.

She breathed heavily and looked away. "I don't know. My parents I guess. They keep saying stuff about . . . that it's wrong to get too serious with someone, and how I'm too young . . . and also stuff like I should be thinking about what I want to do. And college. And how I shouldn't have all my focus on one person."

"And you believe them?" I asked.

"I don't believe *everything*, but they are my parents. I have to believe them about some things."

I sharpened my stick.

"I do want to go to a good college."

I shook my head. "I love you so much," I said. "More than you even know."

"Oh, Pete," she said. She scooted close to me and put her arms around me. I didn't hug her back. I kept my head down, I stayed focused on the stick.

★★★ **43** ★★★

On Saturday I went to Eric Simon's house to meet Jeff Weiland and discuss the future of Mad Skillz. Daniel Fincher, our Mad Skillz drummer, was there when I arrived. I hadn't seen Daniel all summer, so it was nice to see him. Eric led us downstairs to wait for Jeff. The basement looked a lot different. There were new instruments, different drums. Eric had a new guitar. Also there was a big table of computer stuff.

Daniel and I sat on Eric's couch. Jeff was late. Eric kept talking about Jeff and how brilliant he was. He showed us stuff Jeff could do with his computer, like punching up different beats and synthesized rhythm tracks.

Finally Jeff Weiland arrived. He came down the stairs. He was balding and wore tinted sunglasses and a Hawaiian shirt with a suit coat over it. He shook our hands. He acted like this was a momentous occasion, our meeting him.

Eric wanted us to get to know each other. Jeff and Eric pulled up chairs and Jeff told us his vision of the band, how we could still make money playing dances or whatever, but we could do other things as well. What *he* wanted to do was enter us in a World Music competition in Port Townsend. He already had a track completed for the submission. He had everything on it, bass, drums, everything.

"So what do you need us for?" said Daniel.

"To play in the competition," said Jeff, acting slightly offended.

"We're still a live band above everything," added Eric. "It's not like that."

"What kind of bass did you use on the submission track?" I said.

"We didn't use an actual bass," explained Jeff. "It's a synthesized sound that is constructed out of various frequencies to simulate the sound of a bass."

I nodded. Eric and Jeff kept telling us how great it was going to be. I looked at my hands a lot. I asked Eric for a Coke.

That night Margaret called me from Lauren's house. Lauren's brother had bought them some beer, and they were both a little drunk. Lauren was gathering everything Travis had given her and was going to burn it in her backyard. The problem was, he hadn't given her anything. So they decided to burn everything he had ever *touched*, but even that wasn't very much. Lauren finally found a sweater of his. That would do nicely they thought, but Lauren tried it on and decided she liked it and wanted to keep it. Finally, they found a Good Charlotte CD Travis had left there. This they could burn.

Margaret was talking to me on Lauren's cell phone while she followed Lauren around. It was all pretty silly, but I didn't care. It was Margaret's voice in my ear. That was what mattered. I could listen to her for hours.

Then I heard Lauren scream in the background. She had poured lighter fluid on her shoe and accidentally lit herself on fire. Margaret had to drop the phone and spray her with the hose to extinguish the flames.

Later Margaret came back and we talked more. It was all dumb stuff we talked about. It didn't matter. Things were getting right with us again. It was her way of telling me, Be patient, things will work out.

I felt so relieved after that, I went to watch TV with my dad in the living room. He glanced at me when I sat down but he didn't say anything. He was having a drink. There was a Willie Nelson special on CMT.

"Sorry I've been so weird lately," I said, quietly.

"Have you been weird?"

"Yeah," I said, watching the TV. "All this stuff has been happening."

"Like what?"

"Margaret stuff. It's working out though. I think it is."

He nodded.

"Also . . . I kind of got replaced from Tiny Masters," I said.

"Yeah?"

"The original guy is coming back."

"That's too bad," he said. "When did that happen?"

"Last week. I kind of got in a fight with the guitar player."

"You got in a fight?" said my dad. "A real *punching* fight?"

I nodded.

"But you've never been in a fight in your life," he said.

"I know. I wasn't very good at it."

He looked at the TV. He looked back at me. "And you actually hit each other?"

"We tried."

My dad couldn't believe it. "Wow," he said.

"Jeez dad, I'm not a total wuss."

"No. I know. I'm just . . . surprised is all." He looked at the TV. He drank his drink.

★★★ **44** ★★★

At school the next day, I signed up for jazz band again. I needed some sort of gig. Kevin wasn't doing it this year, he was too busy. Seniors usually bailed on jazz band anyway, since it took a lot of time and was considered geeky. Our new drummer was a four-foot-tall black kid, a freshman. His name was Cameron, and he was so short he could barely reach the drums. He was good though. His style was simple and sparse, and he had little tricks, little rhythmic things he did that I had to make him slow down and explain to me. He had obviously played with some good people.

Other than Cameron, jazz band had not attracted a great deal of new talent. A new freshman girl had replaced Jennifer Buckmeyer. Brandon Hughes was back with a new trombone. Pam Olson looked the same but was nicer. She seemed relieved Kevin was gone. A lot of people did. But I missed him. I missed him a lot.

Kevin and I still hung out sometimes. In October, he and I went to see The Lab at an all-ages show downtown. In the crowd were some of the same music people from Sanctuary, and the Summer Fun Band party. It was hard seeing them though. If you weren't in a band you were nothing to those people.

Also in October I had a couple of practices with Mad Skillz. This was totally different from the old Mad Skillz. Before,

Eric always had gigs for us to play. We were always scrambling to learn the latest hits for the dances. Now we had no gigs scheduled. All we did at practice was work on "an original composition" by Jeff Weiland, which was this complicated jazz riff we had to play over and over while he did things on his computer. It was bad. Dan Fincher gave me a ride home after one of them and told me he was going to quit and join a band that played hotels by the airport. They made $250 a night. "You have to play oldies," he said, "but for two-fifty . . ."

Then, the day before Halloween, Lauren's parents suddenly went out of town, and she decided to have a party. It was pretty last-minute, so Margaret and I had to help her get ready. Also we had to invite people. I called Kevin and Robert Hatch and a few other people. I also called Eric Simon and Daniel Fincher, but not Jeff Weiland. I told Kevin to invite any of the music people we had met over the summer. I actually wouldn't have minded seeing Nick Carlisle or Kim again. But I couldn't invite them.

★★★ **45** ★★★

The night of the party, Lauren was pretty nervous. Part of the reason she was having it was to get over Travis. I wasn't sure how getting your house trashed by a bunch of strangers was going to accomplish that. Or worse, having no one show up.

But people came. Robert Hatch got there early with a couple of his buddies. Some of Lauren's new cross-country friends came in a big gang (she was doing cross-country now). Her brother arrived with a couple of his friends who were in college. Then a clique of sophomore girls who I didn't know showed up and started dancing in the living room. They were cute and they must have called people on their cell phones, because a steady stream of boys began to appear, many of them sophomores and even freshmen.

I hung out in the kitchen with Robert Hatch. He didn't really know how to act at a party. He didn't like beer, and he and his friends stood around talking about video games. It was okay though. It was nice to have him there.

At ten-thirty, two carloads of senior guys showed up. They immediately pushed their way to the kitchen and emptied the refrigerator of beer. At eleven, another wave of people appeared, all at once. I guess the word had gotten out. I was in the backyard with Margaret, and you could barely get into the house, it was so crowded. We saw Lauren run by us to the living room where people were dancing. She was dragging Robert Hatch by the hand. She was kind of drunk by now and tripping on things, and I assumed Robert would be embarrassed, but when I watched them, he was smiling— and he actually *danced* with her, even though Lauren was about three inches taller than him.

In the midst of all that, Kevin and Jennifer Buckmeyer arrived. Kevin was very clothes conscious now. He always wore cool T-shirts and vintage jeans. Jennifer was dressed up too. She was doing her eighties look, with her stripped shirt hanging off her shoulder.

Kevin had his own six-pack of Pabst Blue Ribbon beer. He

looked a little bored with everything, but he was a senior so that was natural. Jennifer was nice though and talked to me and Margaret, and it was like we were all old friends, which I guess we were.

★★★ **46** ★★★

At midnight there was a commotion in the backyard. Everyone ran to see. It was two of the seniors who had drunk all the beer. They were dancing shirtless on the picnic table in the rain. One of them was doing a striptease and pulled down his pants, but not his boxers. Another friend tried to jump up too, but the picnic table was slick with rainwater, and he slipped and fell on his ass. His friends immediately poured beer all over him.

This little episode lent a new excitement to the party. Inside, someone turned off the lights and turned up the music, and people really started dancing. The whole house seemed to be vibrating with the beat. It was so fun. Margaret was holding my hand and we lurched into a corner and started making out. She was totally pushing against me and asking where we could be alone.

We ended up in a linen closet upstairs; it was the only place we could find. We made out and did other stuff. It got pretty intense. Then Margaret accidentally leaned against the door, which opened, and we both spilled out into the hall. People saw us, half naked, and started laughing. Margaret screamed with embarrassment and pushed me back in. We laughed and made out some more.

Then things got more serious. Margaret reached up and gripped one of the top shelves. She arched her body toward me. It was so sexy, it was like she was giving herself to me, giving me everything. I never felt closer to her. After all we'd been through, it was the best time ever. Even as people walked by in the hall, just inches away.

Afterward we stumbled down the stairs to the main floor. A lot of people were making out, on the stairs, in the hall. It was turning out to be a great party.

Margaret and I returned to the kitchen. Someone had bought several cases of beer, and Robert was helping Lauren and another girl load it into the refrigerator. Robert was actually drinking a beer himself, which was a strange sight. When they finished that, Lauren took his hand and led him back to the dancing.

"Did you see that?" said Margaret, over the music. "Lauren and Robert are so hooking up!"

"But he has a girlfriend," I said. "In Seattle."

"You can't have a long-distance relationship in high school," scoffed Margaret.

"He thinks he can," I said.

"We'll see what he thinks after this," said Margaret.

We watched them. They danced normal for a second, then Lauren put her wrists on Robert's shoulders and did this slinky dance, slowly working her way forward until their foreheads touched.

"Where'd she learn to do that?" I said to Margaret.

"Lauren is a very sensual person. People don't notice because she's so skinny."

Robert was noticing. His glasses were getting tipped off his head. He was hanging in there though. His hands, clumsy as they were, found their way around her waist. And then he kissed her.

A few minutes later Kevin found us in the kitchen. He had his cell phone in his hand. "Pete, hey, you gotta come outside for a sec," he said.

I had my arm around Margaret. "I'm kind of in the middle of something," I said.

"Dude," he said. There was something very serious in his face.

"All right," I said. I released Margaret and followed him through the crowded living room. Maybe something had happened with him and Jennifer.

We went out the front door. There was nothing outside but a lot of cars and a few people hunched in the rain talking on cell phones. Then I saw a familiar minivan parked across the street. The Carlisle brothers were here.

I swallowed. "What are *they* doing here?"

"C'mon," whispered Kevin. "They want to talk to you."

"About what?"

"Just c'mon."

I followed. We walked to the end of the driveway and across the street. Billy and Nick saw us coming and got out of their car. A twinge of fear shot through me. Was this going to be another fight?

"Hey," Nick said to me.

"Hey," I said, cautiously.

Billy came around the car to our side. I watched him.

"What's up?" said Nick.

"Nothing," I said, taking a breath. "What are you guys doing?"

"Nothing," said Nick. "We wanted to talk to you."

"Yeah?" I said. "What about?" I glanced at Billy.

"You know that night at the Summer Fun Band party?" said Nick. "When you and Billy . . . ?"

I nodded.

"We talked about it," said Nick. "And we respect what you did. You thought you were getting kicked out. And you were pissed off about it."

"I *was* getting kicked out," I said.

Nick nodded his agreement. Billy leaned against the minivan. He hadn't looked at me yet.

"You were willing to fight for your spot," said Nick. "We respect that." He looked at his brother, who said nothing. "Anyway, we want you to come back. Jason isn't working out."

"Jason *sucks*," said Kevin, forcefully.

"Yeah," said Nick. "So anyway, you wanna be back in the band?"

I tried to pretend to think about it. I don't think I fooled anyone. "Yeah," I said. "All right."

"Good," said Nick.

I looked at Billy. He looked at the ground.

"All right," said Kevin. "It's settled. Pete's back on bass. Pete and Billy shake hands."

Billy didn't move. I had to go to him. I walked over and

shook his hand. I looked into his face when I did it. He looked back—he was at least trying to be sincere.

"Okay," said Kevin. He gripped my arm. "Now we got a party to get back to." He pulled me away and steered me up the driveway. I don't know what Nick and Billy did. I was afraid to look behind me.

At the top of the driveway Margaret was waiting for us. Kevin slapped me on the back and left us alone.

"What was that about?" asked Margaret.

I still didn't look behind me. "I'm not sure exactly. Are those guys still standing there?"

"No, they just drove away."

I turned. The minivan was at the end of the block. "Wow," I said quietly. "I think I'm a Tiny Master again."

The Rise of the Tiny Masters

★ ★ ★ **48** ★ ★ ★

One thing about the Carlisle brothers, they worked hard. It was amazing how much they had done in the three months I had been away. They had seven new songs, all of which were better than any of the early stuff. Nick was way more confident on vocals. Billy had developed a hard riffy style, like a metalized surf guitar. Kevin had reduced his drumming from the usual bashing and crashing to a more disciplined precision. A huge part of it, I could see, was confidence. They knew they were good now, and it seemed to give everything they did an extra spark of energy and excitement.

It was clear from the first practice that their cool new songs would need cool new bass parts. I'd never made up my own parts before, not like this. Fortunately, their confidence spread to me. I began to develop a style. I had no choice, the Tiny Masters of Today now had a very specific sound, and I had to find my place within it.

For the next two weeks we practically lived in the Carlisles' basement. I never worked so hard in my life. One night we might struggle for hours over one small part of one song, and the next day we would finish two new songs in an hour. I had thought I was a pro musician before because I made money, but being a pro was not about money. It was about giving up all personal and individual considerations for the good of the group. It was about total commitment to the overall sound.

It was also totally fun. At school, at home, even with Margaret, I spent every waking second thinking about those songs.

Then we went on the road. The last two weeks of November we played five gigs. We played the Sanctuary Sunday all-ages night, this time as co-headliners with The Idiots. We were great. The crowd wasn't very big, but Billy and Nick didn't seem concerned. *Word would get around* was their philosophy.

We played in a bar in Eugene a couple nights later. There were only about twenty people, but we "killed" (as Nick and Billy were fond of saying). That entire trip was a blast, riding down in the minivan, hanging out with the other band, playing Nerf football in the parking lot.

On a Friday night we played at Blackbird in Portland with a popular local band called Lowerarchy. They were college kids, and they had a big following. We opened. At first the audience just stood there, but after a couple songs people were into it. One of our new songs, "Rock Star Superstar" was emerging as our new hit. It was about this poor guy who works at Burger King but in his dreams he's a big star. We played it over again for the encore, and people went crazy. So we played it *again* for our third encore. People sang along with the chorus:

Rock Star Superstar
Doesn't matter where you are
Ride the bus with your guitar

The next weekend we played two nights in Olympia at a college radio festival. The first night we got stuck playing the opening slot, which sucked. It was still fun though. The next day we hung out and met the other bands. The Lab was there, and everyone was talking about them. They had finally signed their record deal. Lowerarchy was getting a lot of buzz too.

On the second night, we had another bad spot. But then one of the organizers changed our place on the order so we could play to a bigger crowd. I guess people had been talking about us. We played in an old movie theater, and it was packed. We killed, of course. We stole the show. People were all over us after that. Suddenly everyone was in our dressing room, everyone wanted to talk and hang out and invite us to parties. We were the center of everything. Just like that. One show. It was so weird. I guess I never really understood what *buzz* meant exactly. I never thought it was real but it was. And we had it. It was all around us.

★ ★ ★ **49** ★ ★ ★

Of course Margaret wasn't too thrilled about me spending weekends in strange cities acting out my rock star fantasies.

"I wanna come next time," she said at school, just before Christmas break.

"You can totally come . . . if those guys say it's okay."

"But they won't. Jennifer Buckmeyer said Billy and Nick wouldn't let her do *anything* with them. They wouldn't let her ride in the van with them. And she used to give them gas money."

"They're just uptight. They take things really seriously."

"And all those girls throwing themselves at you," said Margaret, hitting my knee with hers, under the table.

"Nobody throws themselves at the seventeen-year-old bass player," I said.

Actually some stuff *had* gone on in Olympia. A strange older woman had followed Billy around. She was a massage therapist (supposedly), and she kept asking him to come to her massage studio. She said she had special techniques she wanted to try that would totally relax him. Billy kept avoiding her, but Nick disappeared with her for a couple hours and when he came back he was laughing and saying all the crazy stuff she did to him. He also said that *nothing* that happened on the road was ever to get back to our Portland girlfriends, *ever*. Kevin and I were like, "We would never tell," but you could tell Billy and Nick weren't sure we could be trusted.

My dad was also a little concerned with my new life, especially when I started coming home at midnight every night with no schoolbooks. He never said anything though. I think he liked Tiny Masters a little more, or at least the idea of it, now that I'd stuck up for myself within the group. He never brought it up though. He stuck to the usual parental thing:

you can do it as long as you keep your grades up.

During Christmas break we spent ten days in the Carlisles' basement recording a demo CD that Nick was going to give to a record company in Seattle. That's how it was with Billy and Nick. Kevin and I were just getting used to being a "known" band, while Billy and Nick were three steps ahead, hustling to get us a record deal.

★ ★ ★ **50** ★ ★ ★

The first day back from Christmas break, I went to Mr. Moran's office and told him I was quitting jazz band. He kind of freaked out. When I told him about Tiny Masters he freaked out even more. He warned me that trends in rock never lasted more than three years and that the stuff I learned in jazz band would stay with me my entire musical life. I didn't know what to say to that. I liked Mr. Moran, so I said it was also about my schoolwork; my grades weren't good. Hopefully that made him feel better.

That same week I called Eric and told him I didn't have time for Mad Skillz either. He took it pretty well, considering. He was distracted anyway. He was in the middle of a big fight with Jeff Weiland. Jeff wanted to copyright his "original composition" and they were arguing about what share Eric should get in the rights.

"That sucks," I said. It made me sad to part ways with Eric. Mad Skillz had been fun in its way, and it would always be my first band.

"Daniel's bailing anyway," said Eric. "He's going to join a band that plays at hotels by the airport. I guess it pays pretty good."

"Yeah," I said. "He told me. He said you have to play oldies."

"See? That's the thing," said Eric. "There's always a catch. There's always a compromise in this business. Sometimes I wonder if it's worth the bother."

"Yeah," I said.

"So this band you're in, what sort of stuff you guys doing?"

"Alternative, I guess you'd call it."

"That sounds good."

"It's a lot of traveling though," I said, trying to make him feel better. "You know, it's a lot of college radio stuff. So you gotta hit the colleges."

"Sure. The *cool* people. You guys will probably end up on MTV," he said.

"Who knows," I said.

"Hey man, I hope you guys make it. I really do. It'd be good to see someone with actual talent make it for a change."

I got a lump in my throat when he said that. "Good luck with Jeff and all that," I said and I got off the phone.

A few days later I was in the cafeteria when Cameron, the jazz band drummer came up to me.

"Hey you," he said.

"Hey what?" I said. He was so small it made you smile.

"Where'd you go?" he asked. "Why'd you quit jazz band?"

"I got other commitments."

"What other commitments?"

"I'm in a real band," I said, which sounded snotty, but I figured Cameron would understand.

"Yeah?" he said. He looked like a child, but his face was complicated and smart. "What kind of real band?"

"A rock band. We write our own stuff. We play all over."

"Yeah? You like it?"

"Are you kidding? It's the best."

He watched my face. "I'm gonna be in a real band."

"I'm sure you will be," I said.

"I gotta grow first. My dad says I'll play a lot different when I'm bigger."

"I bet that's true," I said. "Is your dad a musician?"

"My dad's a great jazz trumpet player. He was famous."

"So was my dad."

"I'm gonna be famous."

"Yeah?" I said.

"Are you going to be famous?"

"I don't know."

"If you don't know, you won't be," said Cameron. "My dad says people who are gonna be famous always know."

"Maybe so," I said. "Maybe so."

★★★ **51** ★★★

Meanwhile, all that winter, Robert and Lauren were falling deeper in love. Margaret and I went bowling with them. I watched Robert watch Lauren. He never stopped staring at her. He watched her tie her shoe. He watched her drink her Coke. At one point I elbowed him and told him to stop it. "You're going to creep her out," I told him.

We bowled. Robert took his turn. I took mine. Lauren and Margaret were discussing the latest new couple at school. Allison Greely, Sarah Vandeway's best friend, was going out with a new transfer student named John Stanton. The issue everyone was talking about: was John Stanton now the hottest boy in our class?

Robert didn't like hearing his girlfriend discuss the hotness of other boys. "Would you listen to them?" he complained. "If they like the guy so much why don't they go out with him?"

I nodded my agreement. "Yeah," I said. "I hate girl talk."

"Don't you get jealous?"

"I try not to."

"I don't want to hear about *John Stanton*. . . . " he grumbled.

"Maybe it's good," I said. "Maybe it means you guys are really secure as a couple."

"It's *your turn*, Lauren," he said to her angrily.

"All *right*, Robert," said Lauren, but she didn't stop talking to Margaret.

Two other girls from our school saw us and came over.

They had also heard about Allison Greely and John Stanton. Now all four of them chattered about it.

Robert shook his head with disgust. "I'm going to bowl for her. I can't take this anymore," he said. He got up and searched through the bowling balls.

"I'm *going* Robert!" said Lauren. "Relax!"

Robert came back and flopped on the plastic seat. "God, I hate being in love," he said.

Later the four of us parked on the dark end of the Woodridge Mall parking lot. It was one of the secret make-out places for people at Evergreen. It was Margaret's idea to go there. Robert and Lauren didn't have too many chances to make out. Margaret thought we should leave them alone. So we did, we got out and walked around the empty mall parking lot.

We walked for a long time, without saying anything.

"I got my Stanford catalog today," Margaret finally said.

"What's that?"

"You know, for Stanford University. It's got the application and stuff in it."

"Oh," I said.

"Are you sending away for college stuff?"

"No."

"Maybe there's a music college you could go to, Juilliard or something."

"Juilliard?" I said.

"Or one of the other ones."

"I don't think musicians really need college."

"You can still go. You could study music. Doesn't your dad want you to?"

"I doubt it. He didn't go to college. Doesn't it cost a lot?"

"You can get scholarships. You should at least talk to the counselor at school."

I nodded. We had come to the main entrance of the mall. It was closed and locked.

"Remember when we first came here?" she said. "To get your red high-tops?"

I did. I stared through the glass doors, at the inside of the mall. It was empty and still, but full of light.

"You didn't even want to sit with me on the bus," said Margaret.

"I told you, I was going to sit behind you, so I could put my feet up."

"Don't give me that," she said. "You didn't want to sit with me. I saw the expression on your face."

"That's not how I remember it."

"Don't worry." She slipped her hand inside my arm. "I forgive you."

A voice called somewhere. I heard my name. I turned. Robert was running toward us. He was in a panic of some sort.

He waved frantically at me, then stopped when Margaret turned.

"What's he want?" said Margaret.

"I better go see," I said.

I walked into the parking lot. Robert continued to wave me away from Margaret.

"Hey," he whispered as I got to him. "Do you have any condoms?"

"Dude, are you serious? You guys just started going out."

"It's been two months," he said.

"Two months isn't that long," I said.

"That's what I thought," he whispered, glancing back at the car. "But she seems to want to."

I got out my wallet. "Don't you have any?"

"I did, but I dropped it," he said. "It got dirt on it. Oh God, I'm going to blow this, I just know it."

"Nah, it'll be fine," I said. I had a condom. I pulled it from my wallet and gave it to him.

"So don't come back," he said. "To the car I mean."

"How long is this going to take?" I said.

"How would I know?"

"We have to go home eventually."

"I'm so nervous," he said. "My knees are shaking."

"Don't worry. She's probably nervous too."

"Were you nervous, when you guys first . . . ?"

"Of course. Everyone's nervous," I said. "Just don't take all night."

He took the condom and ran back to the car.

★ ★ ★ **52** ★ ★ ★

In January, Billy and Nick sent our demo CD to the record company guy in Seattle. He called us immediately. He liked the CD, he thought it was fresh and distinctive. He wanted to see us live. He set up a gig for us in Seattle on February 20.

We had other gigs in the meantime. At the end of January we played a Thursday night at Sanctuary. On February 6 we played Blackbird again. Blackbird was becoming our favorite place to play. We had all our best shows there. I told my dad about it and urged him to come, but he had a faculty dinner with the music department at Portland State. He said he'd try to come later.

Margaret came, with Lauren and Robert. The bouncers wouldn't let them in because they weren't twenty-one, so they had to hang out in the parking lot, in the cold. Chelsea and Jennifer Buckmeyer showed up. Chelsea and Billy had broken up, but she still came around sometimes, now that we were getting popular. Over Christmas Billy had been interviewed by the *Portland Edge*. The journalist had asked him about throwing his guitar around, did he always do that? Billy said no, it was just that one time, because of a relationship problem. So of course Chelsea made sure everyone knew that *she* was the relationship problem.

Blackbird was very crowded. People had been hearing about us, and they wanted to see what the fuss was about. We went on and played okay at first, but then we messed up a bunch in the middle of the set. Also, Nick had the flu and he didn't sound too good. We played better as the night went on. Then, near the end of the set, I looked up, and there was my dad. He was way in the back, practically at the back wall. He was nodding his head. I guess he was, I could barely see. A couple of songs later I looked up and he was gone.

Afterward, Margaret and I huddled in the cold minivan.

"Oh my God, my dad finally saw us!" I said.

"That is so cool," said Margaret.

"He probably hated it." I laughed. He probably thinks Billy is the worst guitar player ever."

"He doesn't care. He just wants to see you," said Margaret. "He probably loved it."

Robert Hatch appeared outside the window. He and Lauren had been playing video games across the street. "We're taking off."

"All right," I said.

"You need a ride, Margaret?" asked Robert. We still had to pack up our gear and get our money, among other things.

"Yeah," she said. She kissed me and opened the door.

I caught her hand. "Can't you hang out?" I said.

"I have to go home. I've got a lot of school stuff."

"But it's Friday night."

"You guys are going to be here all night," she said. "And it's freezing."

"We can hurry."

"My parents have been bugging me lately. This is the most important semester for grades and stuff. For college."

"Oh," I said.

"I'll call you tomorrow."

"Okay," I said.

She closed the door and ran to catch up with Lauren and Robert.

★ ★ ★ 53 ★ ★ ★

Two weeks later we left for Seattle on a cold, rainy Friday afternoon. When a band played specifically for record company people, it was called a "showcase." That's what this was. We had spent all week preparing. We had specially designed a forty-minute set. It had our best songs, with special lead-ins and segues. "Rock Star Superstar" would be our last song, since that was now our "hit."

The gig was actually on Saturday night, but Billy and Nick wanted to get there Friday so we would be fresher and more relaxed the day of the show. Nick had some friends in a band house we could crash with.

The drive was quiet and uneventful. Nick and Billy traded off driving while Kevin and I read comic books in the back. At eleven we pulled up beside an old Victorian house. Nick told us it was called Vexer House because originally a band called The Vexers lived there.

We locked the van and went inside. Vexer House was pretty wild. A different band lived there now, as well as other assorted music people. There were band flyers on the walls and musical instruments lying around. There was also an unofficial party going on (you got the feeling there was *always* an unofficial party going on). Some of these people knew Billy and Nick and seemed to think very highly of them. Kevin and I were greeted warmly too. People had heard of us. Even in Seattle. It was a pretty great feeling.

We spent the next four hours hanging out. There were about fifteen people, mostly guys, all dressed very cool. They were drinking beer, smoking cigarettes, talking about the Seattle scene, different bands, who was getting signed, who was sleeping with who. People played a video game on the TV. Occasionally someone would pick up an old battered acoustic guitar off the floor and play something. Kevin and I sat together and didn't say much and tried to act like we partied like this all the time.

Around 3 a.m. people started to crash. Billy and Nick disappeared somewhere. I think Billy had a girlfriend there, or someone who would be his girlfriend for the weekend anyway. He never told Kevin and me what he was doing girl-wise. This super nice girl named Patty eventually took Kevin and me up to the attic where there were a bunch of cushions and pads and old sleeping bags and stuff. It was the official "visiting band crashing area" she explained. There was even a little boom box and a reading lamp.

Kevin and I curled up in the sleeping bags. We both lay quietly in the dark. You could hear the rain falling on the roof above us. I thought about Margaret like I always did, but this time I thought about how different we were becoming. How I was doing stuff like this and she was going home early to study. I wondered what would happen to us as time went on. Junior year was half over. Would we stay together senior year? Before, the thought of breaking up with her seemed totally impossible. It would be the greatest tragedy of my life. But maybe that wasn't necessarily the case. . . .

Then I forgot about Margaret and thought about how great Vexer House was. The bathroom had old vinyl record covers stapled to the wall like wallpaper. Every appliance in the kitchen was covered with band stickers. And people had heard of us. Even here. They thought we were cool. Even though Kevin and I were still kind of geeks. They didn't even care. They liked us anyway!

I loved it all, everything we were doing, practicing all day, driving all night, sleeping in people's attics. Even if we didn't get signed, even if Tiny Masters never got bigger than we were right now, this was *so much fun*. There was nothing in the world I would rather do.

I turned on my side so I could see out the attic window. Raindrops were running down the glass. If Margaret wanted to go to college and get good grades and do the college thing that was fine. That was her life. This was mine.

★ ★ ★ **54** ★ ★ ★

The next morning the four of us went to breakfast and afterward split up to run errands. Nick and Billy went to meet with the record company guy and also to talk to a woman at the University of Washington radio station who was playing the demo version of "Rock Star Superstar" on the air.

Kevin and I were sent to a trendy store to buy me pants. I was still having trouble with the clothes thing, so Kevin was put in charge of finding me something.

Later that afternoon we met at the club we would play at. It was way fancier than I expected. It was super slick and had more of a big-city, music-business vibe than places like Blackbird where we normally played. The sound system was amazing though. And they were already doing sound checks at five in the afternoon, so you knew they were serious.

We moved our gear in and met the other bands. Both of them were pop/punk bands. They seemed like okay guys, but when they did their sound check I couldn't believe how generic they were. Their style and their music was a total rip-off of every other MTV band. I guess they figured that was the best way to get a record contract. The singer of one of the bands kept asking Billy how we got "Rock Star Superstar" on the local college radio. The guy kept saying, "You must know someone. Who is it?" Billy insisted we sent it blind. They just liked it. When the guy finally left, Billy said to me, "How do you explain to someone what originality is?"

After we sound-checked, Nick and Kevin went back to Vexer House. Billy was avoiding the other bands and reading a book called *Beyond Good and Evil* in our dressing room. I had some new corduroy pants that were too tight. I was trying to stretch them out, but I was too nervous to sit around the club, so I wandered outside, into the rain. I found a little café down the street and got a coffee and sat by the window.

That's when I heard an acoustic guitar. It was a minor chord, strummed in a slow arpeggio. I turned. There was another room attached to the café. I hadn't noticed it when I came in. The guitar began to play a song. A female voice began to sing. It was a light, airy voice. It reminded me of something. I got up. I walked to the doorway that divided the two rooms. The second room had a little stage and tables and chairs for an audience. It was completely empty, except for the stage. There, on a plain wooden stool, sat a beautiful black-haired girl. With a guitar.

153

★ ★ ★ 55 ★ ★ ★

"Oh," she said, when she saw me, hesitating in midstrum.

"No, keep playing," I said.

She did. She sang more and played. She had thick wavy black hair; she was slight and pretty and her voice filled the room effortlessly. She sounded like she'd sung forever, like all of time was in her voice. And she was so young. She was as young as I was.

In the middle of the song she stopped. She got off the stool and bent over a little notebook on the floor.

"I better not do this later," she said.

"Do what?" I asked from the doorway.

"Forget the words."

"You're playing here later?"

"Yeah, are you?"

"No. I . . . I'm playing across the street."

"Oh because there's an open mike here. They said I could practice before."

"You sound . . . amazing."

"Really? Thank you. Now if I could only remember the words."

"It doesn't even matter," I said. "You could sing anything."

"That's sweet," she said. She was on her hands and knees beside the stool, turning the pages of her notebook.

I moved into the room. I sat at one of the empty tables in the front.

"So what do you play?" she asked me, still flipping pages.

"Bass."

"Really, so you're in a band?"

"Yeah. We're called the Tiny Masters of Today. It's kind of a weird name but—"

She lifted her head. She stared at me. "You're in Tiny Masters of Today?" she said. "You guys do that song 'Rock Star Superstar.' I love that song."

"You know it?"

"Oh my God, I love it! They've been playing it all week on KUW. 'Ride the bus with your guitar.' I sing that all the time, usually when I'm riding the bus with my guitar," she said, grinning. "Aren't you kind of young though?"

"I'm seventeen," I said. "How old are you?"

"Seventeen."

"How did you start so young?" I said.

"I just did. It's the only thing I ever wanted to do."

"Me too. And my dad's a musician."

"My mom is."

"Wow," I said. "My mom was too. Everyone in our family . . ."

She smiled at me. "What's you name?"

"Peter."

"I'm Cassandra."

"I want to see you play," I said. "When are you going on?"

"I don't know, you have to get on a list. And you have to wait. It's kind of a pain."

"Can you play something right now," I said.

Some other people shuffled into the room. They had acoustic guitars too.

155

Cassandra quickly swung herself back onto the stool. She began a familiar chord progression. She sang:

"Rock Star superstar
Doesn't matter where you are
Ride the bus with your guitar. . . ."

I laughed, and she did too. "I liked your other song better," I said.

"My songs are too sad," she said. "That's what everyone says."

"I love sad songs," I said.

"Me too," said Cassandra.

More people came in. A woman with a clipboard arrived and seemed to want Cassandra to get off the stage.

I helped Cassandra gather her stuff off the floor. She asked me where I was staying.

"This place called Vexer House."

She touched my arm. "Get out! Vexer House? Oh my God, that's the coolest house in Seattle."

"I know, isn't it the best?" I said, excitedly. "We stayed there last night. We partied with them." I glanced at my watch. It was ten after six. We were supposed to be at the club at six. I was late.

"Oh no, I gotta go back," I said. "Can you come see us? I'll put you on the guest list."

"I'd love to, but this usually goes on all night."

"Could you come to Vexer House afterward?"

"Yeah. Totally. I live by there."

"I wish I could stay and listen to you but this gig, it's a showcase, it's kind of important."

"I'll play for you later."

"That would be great," I said, standing up and looking at my watch again. "I really gotta—"

"Go! Go! And good luck! I'll see you later."

★★★ 56 ★★★

I was in a daze as I crossed the street and ran back to the club. It was drizzling now, and a fog had come in off the ocean. Seattle was more oceanlike, I was noticing. Portland smelled like the forest. Seattle smelled like the sea.

No one noticed I was late. Everyone was busy checking out the free stuff that had appeared in the dressing rooms. There was imported beer, fresh fruit, Italian mineral water, all sorts of fancy stuff.

A band called Boys Town went on first. Kevin and I watched them from behind the stage. Boys Town was clean, polished, professional, and sounded exactly like fifty other pop/punk bands. I felt sorry for them that they thought imitating other bands was going to work. But who knew, maybe it would.

We went on at ten-fifteen. Exactly. We played for forty minutes. The crowd was older, but they seemed smart and not totally clueless. They watched and listened and clapped. It wasn't a bunch of old men with cigars like Nick had made it sound like. It seemed okay. I thought we played pretty well.

Billy and Nick seemed disappointed though. They complained that it wasn't really our element.

Afterward I wanted to go back to the café down the street. I told Kevin I had met a folksinger girl there. He raised an eyebrow. "It wasn't like that," I told him. "She's just this awesome girl."

Nick wanted us to stay though, in case the record company guy wanted to meet us. So we did. We had to hang out with Boys Town, who were talking on their cell phones and toweling off and putting their costumes and makeup away. They were so lame, but they didn't care. They wanted a record deal and they were going to do whatever it took.

The record guy never showed up, so we finally went back to Vexer House. It was a relief to be back there again. People were partying. There were a lot of new people, a lot of girls I noticed, most of whom wanted to meet Nick or Billy. As the night continued, a lot more people showed up. I guess people had heard Tiny Masters were there and they wanted to meet us and check us out. Or at least meet Nick and Billy. Kevin was enjoying himself though, talking to some cute girls who were freshmen at UW.

Then I felt something bump me in the back. I turned. It was Cassandra. She was poking me with the end of her guitar case.

A huge smile spread across her face. "Oh my God, look at this crowd!" she said.

"I know," I gushed. "I think they're here for us."

"They totally are, are you kidding? Do you know how big you guys are going to be?"

I didn't, but I liked the sound of it.

I introduced Kevin and Cassandra and we all stood there grinning, me most of all.

"So how was your showcase?" Cassandra asked us.

"It was weird," said Kevin.

"That club has the worst vibe," said Cassandra.

"It seemed like a lot of yuppies," said Kevin.

"Welcome to Seattle!" said Cassandra.

Everyone laughed. Cassandra looked at me. She wanted something, I wasn't sure what.

"Do you want to . . . put your guitar somewhere?" I said.

Kevin gave me the raised eyebrow again.

"Sure," said Cassandra.

"You can put it upstairs with our stuff," I said.

"Okay," she said, shrugging adorably.

★ ★ ★ 57 ★ ★ ★

What happened next was very strange. Before that, I had never been in a situation where I didn't know what I was doing. Like people say, "Oh I got really drunk and I don't remember what I did." Or people say they got carried away doing something and they couldn't stop. That never happened to me. I always knew what I was doing.

But not that night. Cassandra and I walked up the various staircases to the attic to put her guitar away. We tried to make small talk, but nothing we said really made sense. It didn't matter anyway. What was going to happen was going to happen. It was unstoppable.

We were barely three feet inside the attic when we started

making out. We ended up on the floor among the old cushions and the smelly sleeping bags. After a few minutes we managed to stop and compose ourselves. Cassandra straightened her shirt and got out her guitar, like she had originally planned. I found a candle and lit it and we turned off the lights. She tuned her guitar, but before she could start singing we were kissing again. And lying down again. Before I knew it her shirt was off. And my belt was coming undone. It was so unreal. It was like a dream. . . .

Then I came back to myself. Suddenly I was awake again and face-to-face with a girl I didn't know, a girl with a big tattoo on her shoulder and a piercing in her eyebrow, a girl who was about to have sex with me, a total stranger.

"What's the matter?" she said, seeing the change in my face.

"I . . . I just thought of something," I said.

"What?"

"I have a girlfriend," I muttered.

She pushed me off her and sat up. "You do?"

I nodded. "I guess I should have said something. . . ."

She looked at me. She looked at the candle. I couldn't tell if she was mad or not.

"I mean . . ." I stammered.

She turned back toward me. "Well . . . we haven't really done anything . . . if that's what you're worried about."

"I know, I'm just . . . I don't know what to do. I'm so attracted to you," I said quietly.

She smiled. "It's okay," she whispered. "We're just hanging out. It doesn't have to be a big deal." She leaned closer and kissed me gently on the lips. "And we can keep it to our-selves. Nobody has to know."

"Yeah but—" I stammered. "I kind of . . . I love her. My girlfriend I mean. I shouldn't be doing this."

Cassandra pulled back. Her face was soft and perfectly smooth in the candlelight. "You seem like a very loyal per-son," she said.

"I am, I guess. It's stupid I know. You probably think—"

"No, that's okay, if you don't want to."

"Sorry . . ." I muttered. We didn't talk. Eventually we lay down again. She rested her head on my shoulder. I touched her hair and stroked it and we both stared at the candle. The noises of the party came up through the floor. But even lying with her started to feel wrong. She must have sensed this and got up. She packed up her guitar. I sat on the floor, watching her.

"Wow, this turned weird in a hurry," she said.

"I'm sorry," I said.

"It's all right. It's just a little embarrassing is all."

"It's nothing about you," I said. "You're amazing. I'm so glad I met you. Really."

"It's okay," she said, closing her guitar case. "Stuff hap-pens. Maybe I can use it. Maybe I can write a song about it."

She stood up. I stood up too and faced her. She was so beautiful, but she was also old in her face. Not old in years, old in experience, old in the ways of the world. She'd been around. I hadn't noticed that before.

She walked past me to the door. "One thing though," she said, turning back. "If you're going to be in music . . ."

"Yeah?" I said.

"Well . . ." she said, thinking for a moment. "Nothing I guess. You're awfully sweet. And it's hard to stay innocent. I guess the longer you can stay that way, the better."

I nodded.

She did a cute little hand wave and disappeared down the stairs.

Trials

★★★ **58** ★★★

We got back to Portland late on Sunday night. Kevin drove me home from the Carlisles'. Away from Billy and Nick, Kevin relaxed and talked freely. "Dude, what if we get a record contract?" he said. "We're still in high school!"

"That would be so weird," I said.

"It would be *awesome*."

"Yeah," I said. "I'm just glad those guys are dealing with it."

We drove. "So what happened with that Cassandra chick?" said Kevin. "At Vexer House. You guys sort of disappeared."

"We went upstairs."

"I know you did. What happened?"

"She wanted to play me a song," I said.

"Really. She just wanted to play you a song? She looked like she might do more than that."

"Nah. She just played a song."

"Huh," said Kevin. "And how was it?"

"How was what?"

"The song."

"It was okay."

"What was it about?"

I shifted in my seat. "It was just . . . you know, it was a song. I don't remember."

"All right. You don't gotta tell me."

"She played me a song. That's it."

"She was cute," said Kevin. "And she was into you."

"Yeah. Whatever."

"I'm just saying. If we get a record deal, stuff like that is going to happen."

I stared out the window.

"Think about it," he continued. "Where were we a year ago? We were in jazz band. Watching Pam Olson mess up her sax solos. Now we're playing to record executives in Seattle. I mean, come on, you gotta admit how cool that is."

I shrugged and admitted how cool it was.

It was 3:45 in the morning when I got home. My dad was up. He had a drink and was watching a Conan O'Brien repeat.

"Hey," I said. I put my bag down and went into the kitchen to get something to eat.

"How was the showcase?" he said, turning around.

"Pretty good," I said. I poured some raisin bran into a bowl. "They're hopefully going to talk to the record guy this week."

I went into the living room and sat on the couch next to my dad. Conan was introducing a band called Sparta. They had a heavy, dissonant style, kind of like Tiny Masters. My dad turned up the sound, and we both watched them. The song didn't have verses or choruses. It had three parts that rotated around three times. The singer kind of whispered the lyrics, in this spaced-out way. Nick and Billy would have loved it.

My dad was not loving it. "I am really losing touch with what's going on in music," he said.

"Dad, I gotta ask you something—"

"I mean, I understand that being unintelligible is cool, but come on—"

"Dad?"

He looked at me. "What?"

"I kind of . . . met someone. In Seattle."

He didn't understand. "I thought Margaret was your girl-friend?"

"She is. That's the problem."

"Oh," he said.

"This other girl . . . I don't know what happened. She was a folksinger. . . ." I stopped chewing my raisin bran. "There was something about her. . . ."

"Huh," he said.

"I've never done that before. We didn't even do anything, but if Margaret found out, she'd kill me. . . ."

My dad looked at me. He drank some of his drink.

"So what do I do?" I said.

"That's a tough one. I don't know what to tell you."

"You were in bands. What do people do in that situation?"

"I suppose they do what they have to," he said.

"What does that mean?"

"I guess some people don't say anything. They try not to do things like that, but if it happens . . . they don't say anything."

"And they get away with it?"

He gave me a helpless look. "Hey, ask me something I can answer."

I thought about this. I looked at my dad. "Did you ever . . . ?"

"Did I ever what?"

"Nothing," I said. I stuffed more raisin bran in my mouth, but it was dry, there wasn't enough milk. I almost choked on it.

★★★ **59** ★★★

I rode my bike to school the next day. It was cold, but I was too restless to wait for the bus. I went to the bike rack behind the cafeteria. I undid my lock and ran it through my frame and tire.

"Look, it's Peter McGrady," said a girl. I glanced up. It was Allison Greeley. She was standing with two other girls. One of them was Sarah Vandeway.

"Hey, Peter," she said in a flirty voice. I remembered that Allison and John Stanton had broken up.

"Oh . . . hi," I said.

"Are you famous now?" Allison said, grinning.

I looked around. "No," I said. "Who told you that?"

"A girl in my gym class. She said you and Kevin are in a famous band and you're recording a CD." Allison batted her eyelids in a flirty way. Sarah Vandeway watched me without expression.

"Yeah, we might," I said. "Anyone can make a CD though. It doesn't make you famous."

"*I've* never known anyone who made a CD," said Allison.

Was she teasing me? Was she serious? I wasn't sure. I fumbled with my combination lock. I finally snapped it shut and stood up. The three girls stood there smiling at me, almost daring me to do something.

"I gotta . . . get to class," I said. "See ya." I walked away.

"See ya!" said Allison, and the three of them giggled slightly.

I went to my locker. I looked down the hall for any sign of Margaret. On some days I didn't see her until lunch. That happened a lot recently. We'd been together so long, we didn't need to see each other between every class. Robert and Lauren did though. I saw them standing at Lauren's locker. Robert saw me and gave me a little nod.

I did the same. I went to class.

At third period, Margaret came to my locker. She came up behind me. I didn't see her. "Hey!" she said.

"Oh!" I said, startled.

"What's up?" she said.

"Nothing," I said, keeping my eyes down.

"Weren't you going to come say hi?"

"Yeah, of course."

"I didn't see you all weekend. When did you get in?"

"Like, three in the morning."

"What did the record guy say? Did they like you?"

"We don't know yet."

"How was the show?"

"We played okay, not great. The other bands were pretty lame though. We were better than them at least."

"What was the record guy like?"

"I don't know, I didn't really deal with them."

The bell rang. "Well, welcome back!" she said. She smiled and pecked me on the cheek and ran down the hall.

★ ★ ★ 60 ★ ★ ★

"So Lauren and Robert want to go ice-skating," Margaret told me at lunch.

"Okay," I said.

"Like on Friday."

"We're playing Blackbird on Friday."

"How about Saturday?"

"Yeah, Saturday's cool," I said.

"Oh my God, I have to tell you. These two guys in my Spanish class were talking about Tiny Masters."

"They were?"

"One of them had downloaded one of your songs and was playing it for his friend."

"He was? We don't even . . ." But it was probably the demo CD. Kevin must have sent it around.

"And they didn't know who you were, and these other girls said your name and said I was your girlfriend."

"Huh," I said.

"And the girls all looked at me like wasn't I the lucky one."

I smiled. But this sounded weird. Margaret was trying a little too hard to be positive about all this. It wasn't like her. Not that she wasn't supportive, but she wasn't a cheerleader type. She wasn't a groupie, and she wouldn't want people to think of her like that.

Lauren couldn't go ice-skating on Saturday, so we went on Thursday instead. I practiced with Tiny Masters Tuesday and Wednesday, so I was glad to have a break from music stuff.

We went to Lloyd Center and got our skates and goofed around trying to skate. Margaret was a good skater and Lauren was okay, but Robert and I were pretty bad. I could at least stand up. Robert could barely keep his ankles straight.

Afterward we got hot chocolates and sat at a table where you could watch the other skaters. Lauren and Robert went back on the ice so Lauren could teach Robert how to speed up and slow down. Margaret and I stayed at our table.

I played with my stir straw.

Margaret started bumping her knee against mine under the table.

I bumped hers back. She grinned at me.

"We haven't been alone in a week," she whispered to me.

I grinned.

"Maybe we could hang out tonight?" she said.

"Yeah," I said. "I think my dad might be out."

"Actually, we can go in my parents' car."

"You can get the Blazer?"

"Not to drive," she said. "But I can get the keys."

"And then what?"

"And then we go in the garage." She kissed me on my cheek. "Because the car is in the garage." She kissed me again. "And no one ever goes in the garage at night."

I grinned some more. I was turning red. "Okay."

"I miss you, you know. You're always gone, or practicing."

I swallowed. "I know," I said. "I miss you too." She smiled at me and watched Lauren and Robert. She laughed when Robert fell. She yelled something to Lauren. Everyone was having a great time.

Something was wrong though, and not just on my end. Something had changed for Margaret too. I could feel it.

★★★ 61 ★★★

Meanwhile, Nick and Billy waited to hear from the record company guy in Seattle. After a week there was still no word, so Nick started calling him. For two days he tried to get through but the guy was always out. On Wednesday night, after practice, Nick tried again. Kevin and I sat on the couch. Billy stood behind his amp doing something with a screwdriver. Nick dialed the number and went into the laundry room. Suddenly Nick started talking loudly. We couldn't tell what he was saying, but it was definitely the record company guy, you could tell by Nick's voice.

Kevin and I both strained to listen. Even Billy stopped what he was doing.

The loud talking went on for about ten seconds. Then there was silence. Then Nick talked more, his voice a little too high, a little too strained. Then silence again. For a long moment nothing happened. Nick came out of the laundry room. His face had a pale, stricken quality to it. "We didn't get it," he said. "They said they didn't like us as much as they thought."

Kevin sat forward. "How could they not like us? They loved the CD!"

"They said we weren't professional enough. Our stage presentation wasn't professional."

"Not *professional*?" said Kevin, his face contorting slightly. "What? Like those idiots who played with us? Is that what they call professional?"

"They signed Boys Town," said Nick quietly.

"They did *what*?" said Billy.

"*Boys* Town?" I said.

"Tell me you're kidding," said Kevin. "Tell me you're not serious."

"I'm totally serious," said Nick.

Billy stabbed the top of his amp with the screwdriver.

"Maybe my dad's right," I told Margaret on the phone. "Maybe people don't want something new and different. Maybe they just want the same old crap."

"One record guy doesn't mean anything," said Margaret. "There must be other people."

"I guess so. But this band Boys Town. They were the worst MTV rip-off you ever saw."

"Maybe the record people just want to make money."

"Well *obviously* they just want to make money," I snapped.

There was silence on the other end. "It's not my fault," said Margaret. "Don't take it out on me."

"I'm sorry," I said. "I didn't mean that. . . ."

She didn't answer.

"I said I'm sorry," I said.

"You know," she said quietly. "It's not that easy being your girlfriend these days."

"What are you talking about?"

"You're always gone. You don't talk to me the same way. I'm trying so hard not to freak out."

"Why would *you* freak out?"

"Why do you think? You go away all the time. You stay over in different cities. All these different girls are talking about you guys now. It's not like it used to be."

"But I love you."

"I know you do. And I love you too, but things can get so complicated it stops being worth it."

"What's that supposed to mean?"

"I'm just saying, have a little sympathy for me. You know what it's like to hear girls saying stuff about your boyfriend all the time? It's not that easy."

"Would you rather I go back to being a jazz band geek?"

"I don't know. Maybe I would. I liked things then. Maybe it was better then."

★★★ **62** ★★★

We played a Friday night at Sanctuary in mid-March. It was our first weekend headline at Sanctuary. Everyone treated us differently. The soundman who had yelled at us the first time was now running around doing everything we asked. Reverb on the snare, echo on the vocals, six separate drum mikes, so everything would sound perfect.

A new band called Sintilate was one of the opening bands. They were from the suburbs, like us, but they were awfully cocky for an opening band. One of them started moving Billy's amp around, which opening bands are never supposed to do. When Billy saw his amp turned sideways he complained, and one of their roadies fixed it. Billy still wasn't happy. He was in a bad mood anyway. We all felt bad about getting rejected by the record guy—though of course Billy and Nick had instantly activated Plan B, which was convincing a local Portland label to put out the record.

Kevin and I were in the dressing room when Chelsea came in. She was all glammed up with super thick eye makeup and a short skirt and fishnets. She had dyed her hair platinum blonde, which looked pretty slutty, but I guess that's what she wanted. She was with Kim and another girl. The three of them looked like they'd been partying somewhere before.

While the first band played, Margaret arrived with Lauren and Robert. I didn't think I could get them all in, since none of them had a fake ID. I smuggled Margaret in first, having her carry an empty drum case in through the back door. When I went back for Robert and Lauren, Robert decided it wasn't worth it and he'd rather cruise around anyway, since he had his father's car. So he and Lauren took off. Which left Margaret and me.

All that winter and spring Margaret had been dressing less "punk librarian" and more normal, I guess as preparation for college. Or maybe it was her natural personality returning to her after her sophomore-year rebellion. For tonight though, she had tried to look as downtown as possible. She had eye makeup and her headband. Of course she couldn't compete with Chelsea and her friends, but she had tried.

I had to help Kevin set up his drums, so I left Margaret alone. Chelsea and Kim were the only people she knew, so she tried to stand with them by the stage. I could see her trying to talk to them but they wouldn't talk to her. Chelsea had become very snobby lately, which was ridiculous. She had totally dissed Billy and the rest of us, but now that we were getting big, she was back, acting like she was our best friend. She also pretended like she and Billy were just having a fight, and not actually broken up, even though Billy had not talked to her in a month.

It was one of those nights. There was a lot of tension in the air.

Meanwhile, backstage, Sintilate got cockier by the minute. They were taking up all the room in the dressing room, putting their stuff everywhere, and locking the door while they put on their goth makeup. They went on twenty minutes late, and got off even later. Then they pulled the ultimate rock star move of crashing in the dressing room after their set and not moving their equipment right away. They left their one roadie to do it, and he was busy talking to some girls at the front of the stage.

Nick finally told their roadie to get their stuff off, or we'd do it ourselves. When that didn't work Billy went in the dressing room and confronted the band. They just sat there and stared at him. Then their singer said something sarcastic and Billy picked up a beer bottle and threw it right at the guy's head. It exploded about two inches from his right ear, showering him with glass and beer. That got them moving. The stage was clear in ten minutes.

Our set started slow. Everyone was in a bad mood and the crowd looked skeptical. Chelsea wasn't helping things by yelling drunkenly from the side of the stage. But as the night wore on we found our groove. It was like we finally shrugged off all the crap we'd been through lately and just *rocked*. It was like we were escaping into the music. It was like we were *released*. Kevin and I were so dead on we were making stuff up on the spot. Nick was great. Billy was fantastic. The crowd wouldn't let us leave. We did three encores and the soundman finally had to pull the plug so the cops wouldn't come.

Needless to say, Sintilate was long gone.

★★★ **63** ★★★

Afterward, everyone hung out in the dressing room. The mood had totally changed from earlier, everyone was happy, relaxed, exhilarated from the show. As usual I ran back onstage after the last encore to help Kevin with his drums. Sanctuary was not the safest place to leave stuff unattended, especially at closing time. When I got back in the dressing room I noticed Margaret wasn't really talking to anyone. She was standing by herself.

"Hey," I said.

"Hey," she said, smiling at me. She squeezed my arm. "You were great," she said.

"Thanks," I said. Someone handed me a beer and slapped my back with congratulations.

"Do you want to go?" said Margaret.

I didn't actually. I kind of wanted to hang out with everyone and feel that great postgig buzz. "Like right now?" I said.

Margaret nodded. She wasn't enjoying this. "Oh, well. Sure. If you want," I said.

"I mean you can stay if you'd rather," she said. "It's just so late."

"No, you're right, just let me . . ." I pushed through the people and found my bass. Some guy I didn't know was looking at it. "You guys are awesome!" he said drunkenly.

"Thanks," I said.

"Is it true you and the drummer are still in high school?" asked his girlfriend.

"Yeah," I said.

"That's *so cool*," said the guy. "That's what rock and roll is supposed to be about!"

"I guess," I said. I had to push by several more people to get back to Margaret. It was hard with my big bass, and the room being so crowded. Finally I got clear. I followed Margaret out of the dressing room.

She had her dad's Blazer that night. I was not thrilled to be leaving the club, but the Blazer meant we'd at least be able to park somewhere and fool around.

She started the car and drove.

"So are we gonna stop somewhere?" I said, smiling at her.

"Actually I kind of need to get back."

I sighed. I had left the dressing room to ride home with Margaret and now we weren't even going to do anything. When we got off the highway in my neighborhood I pointed to Raleigh Park. "Can we just park for a second?"

She pulled into Raleigh Park and stopped the car.

"Actually," she said. "There's something I think we need to talk about."

"What's that?" I said.

"Just . . . stuff about us. Stuff about our relationship."

"What about it?"

"Like what's going on. And what our future is."

★★★ **64** ★★★

Margaret wanted to break up. She had good reasons. We were changing. We were becoming too different. She wanted to focus on college. Her parents thought high school was a time to meet a lot of different guys. They thought we were too involved. At first she had disagreed, now she thought they might be right.

She also thought it was unhealthy that I was so deep into Tiny Masters.

"That's my life though," I said.

"Yeah but you're not supposed to have a life yet. You're seventeen. You're supposed to still be learning about life."

I sat there and listened to her. It was strange though. This was one of the most important conversations of my life. This was my first girlfriend, breaking up with me, after almost a year of going out. But all I could think was: why couldn't we talk about this some other time? Why had she ruined this great night, our first headlining gig at Sanctuary?

"And those guys are thugs," she said, about Billy and Nick. "Don't you see that?"

"They're ambitious. That's how you have to be," I said.

"Nobody has to be like that," Margaret insisted. "Life isn't that brutal. And if you make it like that, you're making the wrong choices."

I remembered suddenly that Margaret had been going to a therapist. She hadn't told me much about it, just that her parents made her. I had forgotten about it until now.

But whatever. It didn't matter. She was right. Maybe it would be better if we broke up. We had grown apart during the winter. I found myself staring into my lap as the finality of the situation began to sink in. This was it. This was the end. Me and Margaret. Margaret who I didn't want to sit with on the bus. And everything that had happened since. When I thought of it tears formed in my eyes. I found I couldn't look at her. I couldn't look anywhere.

"I still think you're a great person," she was saying. "I just hope you don't end up in a bad place."

"I won't," I said, wiping my eyes.

"But you might," she said. "I'm *serious*. Because you don't have anyone to guide you."

"What does that mean?" I said.

"Just your whole situation. I mean, your dad means well . . ."

That seemed a little personal, and a little outside of her rights of what to say to me. "Don't say stuff about my dad," I said.

"I'm not saying it's his fault."

"I'd prefer you didn't say anything," I said.

"But don't you see . . . ?"

I pointed at the ignition key. "I think we better go now," I told her.

Now she started to cry. "I would do it myself. I try to, but it's not my role. Don't you see? I can't be your mom. I have to look after myself."

"What are you talking about?" I said, angrily. "I never wanted you to be."

She lowered her head.

"I don't need you to be anything to me. All right? I never did. All I needed was a girlfriend," I said. I grabbed for the ignition key and turned it. The engine turned over, but she wasn't giving it gas. "Come on," I told her. "Start the car. I want to go home. And I don't want to carry my bass."

"Peter, don't be mad. Please!"

If she wouldn't drive me home I'd leave. I yanked the door open. I got out. I moved the seat forward and got my bass.

"No!" she said. "Peter, please don't make it like this!"

But I was out. I had my bass. It wasn't that heavy. I could make it home. I slammed the door shut.

"Peter!"

There was a trail that went through the woods toward my house. I started walking. I could hear Margaret crying in her car.

I followed the trail until the car and the parking lot disappeared behind me. The trees were quiet and tall and still. I walked beneath them, my head lowered, my bass at my side like a weapon.

Sessions

★★★ 65 ★★★

In April, Tiny Masters began recording what we hoped would be our first record. The recording studio was in downtown Portland, on the second floor of a loft building. We were doing it with the small local label Nick and Billy had found.

On the first day we met the producers. Phillip was older, in his thirties. He was the main guy. Chip was his assistant. He was twenty-two. He knew Billy and Nick from high school.

The first night we played through all the songs and Phillip started separating them in terms of what order we should record them in. He wrote down a lot of stuff, and he and Billy talked about what kind of sound we wanted.

The second night we recorded parts of "Rock Star Superstar," since that was our "hit" and we wanted to make sure it was fresh and bouncy. They had Kevin and me play our parts separately. Everyone else piled into the little control room to watch us. I don't think Nick and Billy had ever really noticed how good we were before. Phillip was blown away. I heard him say, "Where'd you find these kids?"

"In a high school jazz band," said Billy.

Another thing, the minute I told my dad about recording, he told me stuff to do. Like how to mike the bass amp to get the warmest sound. Or what settings to use, and other tricks, like putting a little bit of duct tape on the very bottom of the bass strings to mute them slightly. He said the old reggae guys used to do that.

It was a weird process, recording. I'd always heard how boring it got, but I really didn't understand until we were doing it. Like some nights I would play through something once, like literally record for three minutes. Then I'd spend the next eight hours standing around, sitting around, walking around the block, walking to Starbucks . . . it was endless.

Also, everything sounded strange. Like we would hear the playbacks and they didn't sound like a CD, or like a song on the radio, they sounded all spaced-out and "taken apart" or something. Like the bass was over here and the drums were over there and it sounded so disconnected you couldn't tell if it was good or not, or if it rocked.

That was the hardest thing. Trying to get excited and really rip into something after you'd just sat through Kevin adjusting his snare drum for two hours. And also sometimes you'd get "the willies." You'd have to play something by yourself, you'd be in the main room, with the headphones on, and the playback on, and everyone crammed into the booth watching you. Phillip would count you in on his fingers and the music would start and you'd have to play some small part, but because everyone was staring at you, you'd screw it up.

Billy was the best at keeping the energy up. He'd go in to record some three-second guitar thing, and turn it into something totally new and fresh. It made you push yourself to be like him.

★ ★ ★ **66** ★ ★ ★

Was I going to school during this time? I guess I was. I was physically present. I slept during English. I slept during Spanish. I tried not to sleep in math because the teacher would send you to the principal. At study hall I went right to the back, got my favorite seat, rolled my sweatshirt into a pillow, and slept. I slept in the library during lunch, which was good because sometimes I would see Margaret in the cafeteria and I hated that. I avoided her as much as possible. I didn't really hang out with Robert Hatch either, since he was always with Lauren.

I was usually awake after lunch, but I spent all my class time thinking up bass parts or writing lyrics. Sometimes Nick's lyrics sucked, so you were always welcome to write stuff and sometimes he would use it, though it was usually only a phrase or a line. The other thing: even though recording was totally boring, it stuck in your mind. You really couldn't think of anything else. Things would come to you in the oddest places, like right in the middle of the *Canterbury Tales* I suddenly thought of a cool ending for a new song. I had to run to the bathroom to write it down.

One day in the library I was crashed on one of the couches,

half-asleep and humming through a part of a song. I felt something tickle my nose. I opened my eyes. Allison Greeley was touching my face with a piece of string. I jumped and she and Sarah Vandeway and Brittney Plummer all laughed. I sat up and looked at them, assuming they would run off. But they stayed. They actually wanted to talk to me. They asked me about Tiny Masters. Were we really recording an album? I said we were, and they were totally impressed. The three of us talked more. Sarah and Brittney eventually left but Allison sat down on the couch and kept talking. She was telling me what bands she liked and how this guy she knew wanted to start a band but he wasn't a real musician, not like me.

The bell rang and we had to go to class. We left the library together. I couldn't believe it. People were seeing us together. And then, as we parted, she looked back and waved at me. Right in front of everyone.

The recording was only supposed to last three weeks, but when our record label guy heard the playbacks, he really liked them and he and Phillip and Billy worked out a deal to record for another week, to make sure everything was as polished as possible. It would still be a pretty rough recording by major label standards, but a lot of great records were rough. I was starting to notice that, now that I was hearing what went on in the studio. A lot of great albums were actually demos or of demo quality. Hendrix, early Metallica, Nirvana's first record. Having a raw recording was not the end of the world. It was the playing that mattered. If a band was truly good it always came through.

+++

On May 10 we had our last day in the studio. It was sad leaving there. We took our time packing up. You felt like you'd left part of yourself in those tiny rooms.

Fortunately Nick had gigs for us. We played a big party at the All Girl Summer Fun Band house and did the Olympia Pop festival again. It was all fun, no-pressure stuff. In Olympia I even hung out one night with a girl drummer in a band from San Francisco. Her name was Sheila. Nothing happened, but it was good to think about a girl other than Margaret. Not that I thought about Margaret that much. I was too busy. But occasionally during the recording, I had nights where I came home late and wanted to call her and tell her about stuff. And sometimes I would miss her physically and I would think, why did I let her go so easily? Why hadn't I tried to get her back? Other times I knew it was over and so many other things were happening, it was for the best.

At the beginning of June, school let out. I actually went to graduation. Jennifer Buckmeyer wanted me to, since Kevin was graduating. It was weird. All these seniors I had known all this time, finishing, leaving, getting on with their lives. And everyone in the parking lot, celebrating and taking pictures. Kevin seemed to revert to his old self, laughing, clowning around with his senior friends. That part was fun. Jennifer was sort of sad though. She loved Kevin so much. They would still be together of course. She would be a senior next year, with me. Kevin would still be around, playing in Tiny Masters. He was going to take classes at Portland State. It all sounded good and stable and like things wouldn't change. But of course they would.

★★★ 67 ★★★

I took a couple of shifts at Pedro's for the summer. I had to be careful to not overcommit myself. Tiny Masters came first. Other than that, it was going to be a difficult summer. No Margaret, no hanging out at Lauren's, no going to Nature First. I kind of didn't know what to do with myself. I started taking the bus downtown occasionally, and hanging out at 360 Vinyl, which was a record store where the other downtown musicians sometimes hung out. They had several local records there. And one of the All Girl Summer Fun Band girls worked there part-time.

Then one night I came home and found a message on my answering machine. It was Allison Greeley. I was shocked. I started the message over and crouched down to listen. She sounded a little drunk. She wondered how I was and talked about a party she went to and a girl she didn't like and then asked what I was doing over the summer and if I wanted to hang out sometime. She left her number and I wrote it down. I listened to the message again. I listened to it three times and saved it. But could I call her back? My hands were sweating so much I rubbed them on my pants. I looked at the phone. I had to do it right away. If I waited I'd totally psyche myself out. *Don't think. Just do it.* I picked up the phone. My heart immediately began to race. I dialed the number anyway.

"Hello?" said a female voice.

"Hey," I said, sucking in my breath. "Allison? What's up?"

"Pete? Petey?" she said. "Oh my God. It's you."

"I got your message," I said, my voice quavering. "What's up?"

"*Nuh*-thing," she said. "I just felt like talking to you. You don't mind that I called, do you?"

"No, no," I said. "I'm . . . glad."

"Did you hear about what happened at Sarah's party?"

I hadn't. She told me. It was a long complicated story, thank God. Eventually she talked about other things, how vegan diets make you fart, how the new pants she bought gave her a rash, how her friends all had text messaging on their cell phones but she didn't. She was funny and strange and she knew a lot of gossip. I mostly listened.

"So what happened with you and *Mahr*-garet?" she finally asked.

"Nothing," I said. "We broke up."

"She was in my English class sophomore year. She got an A on every paper."

"Yeah, she's like that," I said.

"Do you still love her?"

"Yeah," I said, honestly. "I guess I'll always love her but it's good we broke up. It wasn't working out."

"So you could like someone else now?"

"I guess so."

"Well, that's good," she said.

There was an awkward silence.

"So like, will you call me sometime?" she asked.

"Yeah, totally."

"Are you shy? Some guys are. That's okay. How about I'll call you sometimes, and you call me sometimes?"

"Okay."

A week later I went to a party with Allison Greeley. It was at Sonya Taylor's house. The Taylors were rich and Sonya was one of the most popular girls at our school, so going to her house was a pretty big deal. I didn't know if that crowd would accept me, even though I was definitely more "known" now. People were into Tiny Masters. Kevin was burning our demo CD for people, and everyone had "Rock Star Superstar" on their iPods. Still, I was nervous about going.

Once we got there, it wasn't a matter of being accepted or not. The whole "popular people" world was a lot different than I expected. For one thing, it wasn't very organized. It was just a bunch of stray people. No one cared or even noticed I was there except maybe Sarah Vandeway and Brittney, who were Allison's best friends.

Another thing, it wasn't very crowded. It wasn't like one of those mobbed beer parties like Lauren had. Sonya Taylor's house was big and super nice and so people didn't run around or get crazy. They mostly just hung out and drank and smoked pot outside by the pool.

Allison and I wandered around. We hung out downstairs with Sarah and Brittney for a while. I had always assumed Allison sucked up to Sarah Vandeway, since Sarah was the hottest girl in our class, but she didn't at all. The three of them constantly argued and fought about the dumbest things. Like whose turn it was to get another beer. And which bathing suits were the best. I was surprised. I had always thought popular people were really careful to maintain their popularity, but nobody seemed to care about anything. They just sat around and drank. They didn't even notice they were popular.

Later that night Allison and I went into a bedroom upstairs and made out and did other stuff. She was a very sexual person and not embarrassed at all. At one point she started sucking on my fingers as if she were, you know, doing *that*. I mean, it was great and everything. But it was weird.

After that Allison was my girlfriend. It was an odd relationship. Mostly, we talked on the phone. She would call me at odd times from her cell phone, usually to kill time while she was waiting for a ride, or hanging out with Sarah, or trying on clothes at the mall. She also called me late at night from her bedroom and would ramble and say weird things like, "Isn't Brittney's ass sexy?" Sometimes she would ramble so much I wasn't even sure what she was talking about. She wasn't like Margaret, who was artistic but very structured in the way her brain worked. Allison was totally scatterbrained, which led to problems sometimes. Like she would totally contradict herself, but if you mentioned it, she would get annoyed and be like what-*ever*.

Another difficult thing was: she really thought of me as a rock star. Like sometimes I would be talking about something other than music and she would stop listening to me because it didn't fit her idea of me as a musician. Also, she thought it was cool my dad was in bands and stuff but the moment I told her about my mom and the rest of my family, she made it clear she didn't want to talk about it. In a way I understood.

193

Her parents were divorced and she had her own problems and she didn't want to talk about those either. Still, it felt strange. Maybe that was the thing about popular people, they were good at avoiding the bad things in life. They concentrated on the good stuff: being popular or pretty or having a rock star boyfriend.

★★★ **68** ★★★

"So that's your new girl?" asked Billy one night. We were watching Allison and Brittney Plummer from behind the stage at Blackbird. Unlike Margaret and Lauren, Allison and Brittney had fake IDs. They didn't have to wait outside like Margaret did. They went straight to the bar and got beer.

"Yeah, that's her," I answered.

"Looks like you traded up," he said.

"Yeah, maybe," I said.

"You don't like her as much as Margaret?" he asked.

"It's hard to tell," I said. "We just started going out."

Billy nodded. "She's hot. That other one's cute too," he said. "What was her name?"

"Brittney."

"She have a boyfriend?"

"Not that I know of," I said, though I didn't like the idea of Billy hitting on my girlfriend's friends.

Billy didn't pursue it. He went behind the stage. I waved to Allison at the bar. She and Brittney waved back.

+++

Later, while we waited to go on, I found Kevin and Jennifer in the Carlisles' minivan. Jennifer had cut all her hair off and dyed it blonde. Chelsea had helped her do it. They were hanging out now, Jennifer and Chelsea. Kevin had also dyed his hair. It was part of his idea of "total commitment," which was becoming his catchphrase for not going to college. He wanted to play in Tiny Masters full-time. His parents were not happy about this plan, needless to say.

Jennifer was eating Skittles in the front passenger seat. Kevin sat in the driver's. I flopped in the backseat. Jennifer turned to face me. "Did Allison come?"

"Yeah, she's with Brittney Plummer. They're at the bar. They have fake IDs."

"How's it going with you guys?"

"All right."

"She seems to like you."

"I guess. She calls me a lot. When she's bored."

"Do you like her?"

"Of course. She's Allison Greely."

"So, like, if Margaret had a new boyfriend, would you want to know about it?"

"*What?*" I said, sitting up.

Jennifer looked at Kevin "You probably wouldn't, would you," she said, sounding sorry she had brought it up.

"She's going out with someone?" I said. "Who? Tell me!"

"Oh God, I shouldn't have said anything," said Jennifer.

"Who is it?"

"I shouldn't—"

"Jennifer," I pleaded. "Tell me, you have to."

195

"*Man*," said Kevin, shaking his head.

"Oh God," said Jennifer. "I totally shouldn't have . . ."

"Tell me!"

"It's that guy . . ." said Jennifer. "That guy Brian, who works at the mall."

"Brian Footlocker?"

She nodded.

"Who told you that?" I asked.

"Lauren." She filled her hand with Skittles and poured them into her mouth. "She told me to tell you."

I sat back. I looked at the ceiling of the minivan and blew out a long deep breath.

"She said someone should tell you. And they thought me or Kevin . . ."

Kevin shook his head. "This was not my idea, bro. I can promise you that."

"Well he needs to know," Jennifer said to Kevin.

"Brian Footlocker," I murmured to myself. That shouldn't have surprised me. Of course it was Brian Footlocker. He totally liked her. And she liked him. Had they hooked up last summer at some point? I thought about the night we went skinny-dipping, how comfortable they seemed with each other. Something had been going on. I *knew* it. Not that it mattered. Not that it made any difference now.

Still, I couldn't stop thinking about it.

We played. It was very hot inside Blackbird. The place was packed. Allison and Brittney, beers in hand, pushed their way to the front and went crazy during the first song, whipping their heads around, crashing into people, almost getting in a fight with some punk girls who were trying to look sullen and gloomy.

Afterward I went home with Allison. She was drunk and laughing as we went into her house. Her mother was out of town, so the house was empty except for her older sister who was home from college and watched cable movies all night.

We went into Allison's room. Allison had been bugging me for sex since we started going out. She had already had sex with several other guys. I had hesitated, waiting until I felt more comfortable.

I didn't wait now. We went straight to her bedroom, and straight to her bed. When Allison realized what was happening she breathed sexily into my ear, telling me to hurry, to go for it, she wanted to, she loved me.

She didn't love me, but that didn't matter. This was about Margaret. It was a terrible moment. It was not a good reason to have sex with someone, but I did it anyway. I had to.

★★★ **69** ★★★

The next day I went to the mall to confront Margaret. I hadn't spoken to her since we broke up. I had seen her in the hall at school, we had even exchanged solemn smiles, but once summer started, there had been no contact.

I parked my bike outside the mall. I went to Nature First. She was there, behind the counter, ringing up a customer. She looked good. She was wearing a cute summer dress I hadn't seen before.

I suddenly got nervous. I couldn't look at her but I kept

197

moving forward. A large woman with kids was next in line and I stood behind her. I put my hands in my pockets. I was wearing my "Brooklyn Truckstop" T-shirt, and my cool jeans. That's what I wore all the time now. Also Jennifer had cut my hair a couple weeks before in the bedhead style all the musicians wore. So I looked pretty cool. I hoped I did.

"Hey," said Margaret, when the woman was gone.

"Hey," I said. Neither of us was making eye contact.

"What are you doing here?" she said.

"I heard some things."

"Like what?"

"I heard you were with Brian Footlocker," I said quietly.

"His name is Monroe. Brian Monroe. And what about it? You're with someone."

I looked around the store. There were people in the aisles. I was worried they might come up to the counter.

"Were you guys doing stuff last summer?" I asked.

"What do you mean?"

"You know, last summer, you always hung out with those guys."

"You mean, was I *cheating* on you?"

"Yeah," I said. I finally dared to look at her.

"*No*. God! What kind of person do you think I am?"

I shrugged.

"I can't believe you would say that," she said. "That you would *accuse* me of that!"

"You were so into him though."

"I loved *you*. I never loved anyone else," she hissed at me. "Are you crazy? You were my *first* boyfriend. Do you know how sacred that is to a girl? Do you have any idea?"

I stared at the Nutribars on the shelf below the counter. "But he liked you," I said. "He was into you."

"He wasn't *into* me," she looked hard at me. "He barely likes me now. God, I can't believe you."

I stood there. I had my hands in my back pockets. It was the way Billy stood sometimes. "But what about when we went skinny-dipping?" I said.

"What about it?"

"You guys were like . . . "

"What?"

"I dunno," I said. I was starting to feel hot in my face. And in my brain. I hadn't slept at all the night before.

"What's wrong with you anyway. Coming in here," she said. "You look terrible. Did you and Billy beat someone up? Or kill someone? Are you all on drugs now?"

I shook my head. I suddenly felt very tired.

"And how's *Allison Greeley*. God, of all the people you could go out with after me," she said, slamming her cash register shut.

I stood looking at the Nutribars. A customer appeared. He stepped around me to the counter. Margaret began to ring up his purchases.

I turned and found myself walking out.

Margaret didn't say anything. She didn't try to stop me. From the entrance, I looked back. She was scanning the prices into her cash register. She was acting professional, but underneath it she was still furious. I could tell by her lips. I could read her face. I knew that face *so well* . . . .

Some grade school girls walked into me. They giggled and kept going. I kept going too.

★★★ 70 ★★★

All that spring and summer, Nick had been calling people and sending out our demo in hopes of getting major labels interested in Tiny Masters. One Seattle guy told him we should try to get a manager first. He recommended the Silverlake Management Group in Los Angeles. They did a lot of new bands.

Nick sent them a CD and a week later they called. They wanted us to come down to LA to meet with them. They scheduled a showcase gig for us. Nick immediately started working the phones to arrange the trip. He got us places to stay and a couple of warm-up gigs. The whole thing grew into a little LA mini-tour. We had three gigs: August 9 and 11, and on August 14, the showcase.

"All roads lead to LA," my dad said, when I told him.

"Did you go there a lot?"

"All the time. You had to. There were no industry people in Seattle in those days. It was LA and New York. That was it."

"Nick says it's the big leagues."

"He's right."

"But are we ready for the big leagues?" I said.

"I guess you'll find out," said my dad.

Tiny Masters began rehearsing for the LA shows in mid-July. We were playing two or three gigs a week anyway, but Nick and Billy wanted to get the showcase set honed to perfection.

So we rehearsed two and three nights a week, which made it hard to see Allison. She was taking a yoga class with Brittney and Sarah two nights a week. I was still working at Pedro's a couple of nights a week as well.

We could still see each other during the day sometimes, but my latest realization about Allison was that besides having no attention span, she was a sex maniac. Once we started having sex that's all she wanted to do. Even in the daytime. Even when her mom was right downstairs.

At the end of July, Robert called. We had barely talked during the summer. He invited me to come play Ultimate with some of his friends. At first I wasn't sure I wanted to, but he mentioned seeing Margaret recently. Of course I wanted to hear about that. So I went.

"So what's up with you?" Robert said to me as we sat on the grass after the game.

"Nothing. Just playing all the time. We're going to LA."

"You guys are so serious."

"It's Nick and Billy. They're the serious ones."

"Still," said Robert. "I wish I had something like that."

We watched two guys throw the Frisbee. "So how's Margaret?" I said to him.

"She's okay."

"What's up with Brian Footlocker?" I asked.

"They're going out. I don't know how serious it is."

"She really likes him?"

"I guess so," said Robert. "She's chased him enough. Lauren says it's part of this perfection thing she has. Like

201

everything about him is right for her. The way he dresses, the stuff he likes, supposedly he wants to go back east for college. So on the surface, he's perfect."

"It makes sense, I guess."

"It doesn't though. Because the guy's a flake. Lauren thinks Margaret still likes you, she just won't admit it."

"No," I said. "She doesn't like me. Trust me on that."

"Maybe," he said. "She was kind of a mess when you guys broke up."

I thought about that. I watched the Frisbee float by.

Allison and I were in her bedroom when I told her about the trip to LA. She was not happy. I was surprised. I thought she would think it was cool. Trips to LA were what rock stars did.

"But what am *I* supposed to do?" she said.

"What do you mean?"

"While you're gone."

"I don't know," I said. "Wait for me?"

She frowned. She put on her bra.

"Is there a problem with that?" I said.

"I just. . . . It hasn't been the best summer for me you know."

I watched her. She had the most beautiful skin. I was always so preoccupied with her popularity, I sometimes forgot how good-looking she was.

"We never hang out with anyone," she said. "I never see my friends. Do you even *like* my friends?"

"Of course. I just don't know them that well."

"You don't care anyway. All you care about is your band."

"That's not true."

"What did you and *Mahr*-gret do all the time?"

"We just . . . hung out."

"Hanging out is boring though. I want to do stuff."

"Like what?"

"I don't know."

I sat on the bed. She put on her shirt and buttoned it. Her fingers were small and delicate. Her blonde hair hung in her face.

"I think we should break up," she said.

"You do?"

"Yes," she said.

I opened my mouth to speak but nothing came out.

She didn't look at me. She turned her back to me while she pulled on her pants. She turned sideways and zipped them up.

I rode my bike to Kevin's house. It was a plain one-story house in one of the developments near school. I rang the bell and he came to the door. He was wearing cutoffs and no shirt. Jennifer appeared behind him.

"What's up?" said Kevin.

"Allison broke up with me."

"Oh *Pete*," said Jennifer.

"Come on in," said Kevin.

My dad helped me pack for LA. "Lots of underwear" was his main advice. "You can never have enough underwear."

I had my bag on the kitchen table. I dug through my laundry, which was piled on a chair. I found three more pairs of boxers and put them in my bag.

"And be careful," he told me from the couch.

I nodded. "I'll be with those guys," I said.

"No, it'll be fun, I'm just saying, it can be tough down there. It's a showbiz city. Stuff can happen in places like that."

"Yeah?" I said. "Like what?"

"People change. Especially when money is involved. Especially for bands coming from small towns."

"Portland isn't a small town though."

"It'll seem pretty small when you're down there."

"We're just talking to them anyway," I said. "And Nick and Billy seem to know what they're doing."

"Just keep your wits about you."

"I will," I said. "I'll call if anything happens. Or if some-one wants us to sign something."

"Call anyway," he said. "Let me know what's happening."

"I will," I said.

Los Angeles

★★★ 72 ★★★

Tiny Masters left Portland at ten in the morning. We drove all day and slept in a rest area outside Sacramento. Billy and Nick had borrowed a van from their uncle so we could sleep in it. This turned out to be a bad idea. At night the van was incredibly hot and stuffy; I woke up at 5 a.m., sweating, with a guitar case jabbing me in the back. Billy was sleeping outside, in a sleeping bag in the bushes. Nick was on top of the bass amp. Kevin was next to me, face to feet, meaning his feet in my face. It was so uncomfortable, I crawled outside and lay down on one of the wooden benches by the rest rooms. I fell asleep for an hour and was woken up by somebody's dog, licking my face.

It didn't matter though, as soon as we'd had breakfast and were on the road we were all psyched again. We were in Southern California now: palm trees, pale desert, flashy sports cars passing us at ninety mph. We drove all day, and the closer we got, the more cars there were and the wider the highway became. At six in the afternoon we drove under a gigantic highway sign that said Los Angeles and had six arrows pointing to six lanes. *Six lanes.* It made you understand: LA was the big time. It was the center of everything. We looked at the sign in awe. Kevin took a picture of it.

Then we got lost. We were looking for Venice Beach where a friend of Billy's lived. We were going to park the van and crash on the floor for a couple days. When we finally found it, Billy's friend was having a party. Or his friends were. The guy Billy knew was passed out in the bathroom while several creepy surfer guys trashed his house and smoked his weed. It was not a good situation. But Kevin and I were too excited to care. We left Billy and Nick to deal with them and went for a walk on Venice Beach. It was quite a scene, with all the beach freaks and the tourists and the bums. We found a bar where a blues band was playing. We sat outside and some girls started talking to us. They were nice but seemed skeptical of our chances as a band freshly arrived from Portland, Oregon. That was okay. We got some beer from their car and walked around. It was such a beautiful night. The air smelled like sand and the ocean. There were palm trees and the moon was out and in the background was the gentle sound of waves washing up the beach. It was like paradise.

Billy's Venice Beach friends were too skanky, so the next night Nick and Billy made some calls and found the guys from The Lab, the Portland band that had recently relocated to LA to record their major label debut. They were recording in Hollywood and had rented a little house near the studio. We went there. We were glad to see some familiar faces. They seemed happy to see us as well. It was a little weird though. We had looked up to them so much in Portland as the band that got signed and moved to LA. But they looked worn out and a little . . . well, not as good as you were supposed to look when you were recording your first record.

They seemed relieved to have some company. And they had plenty of room: there were couches for Billy and Nick and a little storage room where Kevin and I could spread out our sleeping bags. So everything was set. We had found our temporary home.

★★★ **73** ★★★

The next day we went to the office of the Silverlake Management Group. We dressed up in our best cool musician clothes. Billy wore sunglasses, as did Nick. I didn't have any, so we stopped at a tourist place on Sunset and got some for me.

We found our way to a sleek glass building in Beverly Hills. Billy told Kevin and me to keep quiet and let them do the talking. Like we needed to be told. We went in and sat in the reception office. Everyone there was squeaky clean and perfectly dressed. After a half hour, they sent us into a large meeting room with a thick oak table. We sat for a while and a woman came in and offered us drinks. Nick made everyone get an Evian water, except Billy, who had iced tea.

Eventually a man and a woman came in. These were the real people. They were dressed casual—but not really. The guy was wearing jeans and a blue shirt, but his hair was perfect and his skin glowed liked he'd just come out of a sauna. The woman was more formal. She had a skirt and a conservative haircut. She had a hard look about her—like she definitely did not want to be spoken to.

The guy's name was Chris Houghton. Nick knew him from talking on the phone. Now the rest of us were introduced. Chris said hi but didn't shake our hands. He took a seat at the head of the table, like the dad of the family. It was kind of funny. I mean it wasn't. It was scary really. But whatever, I didn't have to talk.

Chris started the discussion. He wanted to be completely upfront about everything. This was where things stood: he had the CD. He had listened to it. He liked it. He wanted to listen to it more and get feedback from his colleagues. His primary concern was the total package. He wanted to get to know us, get to know our music, get to know our stage act. He wanted to thoroughly understand the product, so they could make "an informed decision" about whether they would represent us or not.

The woman, Martha, didn't speak. Later, Nick told us she was a vice president, and that's how she checked people out, she let Chris do the talking, then she made the final decision.

After Chris talked for a while he asked us if we had any questions. Nick asked about the showcase gig. Chris didn't know anything. He was flying to New York in the morning, and we would have to talk to his assistant. Billy asked about the percentages. Chris gave a long complicated answer that translated to *we'll see*.

We had no more questions. Ten minutes of sitting at the table and we were done. We got back in our van and drove back to Hollywood.

That night the guys from The Lab took us to a party. It was mostly music people and there was lots of talk about managers and clubs and record deals. People seemed kind of paranoid, like they wanted to know who you were, who you knew, who your manager was. That was LA, I guess.

The party was still fun. People were swimming naked in the pool. Kevin and I did tequila shots with some guys who had moved there from Minneapolis. The band they had come with had broken up. Several members had gone home. "They missed Minneapolis," said the guy. "We used to be big there. They figured better to be local celebrities in Minnesota than nobodies in LA."

Billy met a cute red-haired girl and disappeared. Nick made friends with some guys who knew someone at a different management company. He was good at meeting people like that.

Hours later, Billy reappeared. He told us this crazy story about how the red-haired girl took him to her house. She was a Wiccan and wanted to do weird sex rituals with him. We all had a laugh about that.

We were laughing at everything by that point. We were so fried. It had been a pretty intense day. When we got back to the Lab House, Kevin and I went straight to our storage room and crawled deep in our sleeping bags. We were asleep in seconds.

★★★ 74 ★★★

Nick had been smart to get us some warm-up gigs. LA was fun, but it also wore you down and messed with your head. It was good we would play a couple times before the actual showcase.

Our first gig was at a place called the Vat. It was a small cement room at the end of a strip mall. The neighborhood was supposed to be hip or cool, but it looked like everywhere else in LA, lots of cement and parking lots and cars. And of course you never saw actual people walking around. They were all driving.

There seemed to be nobody in charge at the Vat. There was no one working the sound; a guy showed up at one point to take money at the door, but there was very little money to take and he disappeared again. Oddly enough, the two girls Kevin and I had met in Venice Beach showed up. One of the guys from the Lab came with a friend, though they made a point of looking bored and uninterested and "above" places like the Vat. The other bands were tweaked-out LA types, meaning they were dressed cool but were so sketchy you were afraid they might steal your stuff. Their fan base was as sparse as ours, a girlfriend, a couple of stray friends. There were never more than twenty people in the room.

We were the second of three bands. I was psyched when we went on. I didn't care that there was no audience. I just wanted to play. It went pretty well considering the situation. You could feel the strain of things in the music though. We were pressing a little for the first couple songs. We calmed down though. It was a good warm-up.

During the last band, I went outside with Kevin. We stood in the middle of the deserted parking lot. There was not a single person anywhere. On the main road beyond the parking lot, cars streamed by. It was like watching insects.

"LA is so weird," I said.

"I know," he said. "It's like this huge city. But where is everyone?"

"I feel sorry for the bands here."

We stood watching the cars go by. "Do you think we'll get signed?" he asked me.

"I don't know," I said. "I guess we'll find out."

"Everyone we meet is trying to do what we're doing," said Kevin. "And they all seem so desperate. I wonder if we seem like that."

"We're good though."

"Yeah but a lot of bands are good."

"I know," I said.

"It's probably better not to think about it," he said.

"Yeah, I guess we just gotta do our best. And see what happens."

After we packed up, the Venice Beach girls were still around and they wanted to party. I wasn't sure what to do with them, but Billy had taken an interest in the taller one, so it wasn't my problem anymore. They followed us back to the Lab house. Billy and the tall girl hooked up, which made Kevin mad, not that he wanted her, but we had found them. They

213

were sort of "our girls." It made Kevin uncomfortable that Billy would move in like that. But what could he do? We crawled into our sleeping bags and crashed.

★★★ 75 ★★★

In the morning, something was up. Nick and Billy were stone silent in the kitchen. I thought it might be something about the girls, but they were long gone. No, it was something about the management people. Nick had called them, to check in with the assistant, and there was a problem. Nick wouldn't tell Kevin and me exactly what it was, but he thought they could straighten it out. We had another warm-up gig in two days and then the showcase. Nick said we should all focus on that.

The next day we went with the Lab guys to watch them record. The recording studio was this legendary place, where Nirvana had supposedly recorded parts of *In Utero*. But it was this tiny, smelly little room, not even as nice as the place we recorded in Portland. And the studio people were horrible. They were mean and impatient and when the Lab guy broke something on his amp, they totally didn't try to help. They were like, "It's not our problem, we get paid by the hour," and they went outside and smoked cigarettes.

The next day, we had nothing to do, so Kevin and I walked to Melrose Avenue. We went to a Starbucks where we sat outside and started talking to three girls. It was funny how easy it was to meet girls in LA. Maybe it was something about Kevin and me, we looked so nice and normal. People felt like they could trust us. Maybe we reminded them of their hometown. We told the girls we were in a band and they thought that was great. Kevin took pictures of them and they invited us to come swimming at their pool later.

On Friday we found out our second warm-up gig was cancelled. The club had shut down. To make up for it, we set up and played our set at the Lab house. We wanted to stay tight for the showcase.

On Saturday Billy and Nick went to look at amplifiers and Kevin and I went for a walk down the Sunset Strip. Kevin was convinced we could meet girls anywhere now. We tried to talk to two girls at a magazine stand, but they grimaced and turned their backs. Then we went to Tower Records. I asked a girl who worked there if she had ever heard of the Tiny Masters of Today.

"No, who are they?"

"It's this great band from Portland, Oregon. They have a CD you can download."

Her eyes glazed over. "Let me guess," she said. "You're in this band."

"Me?" I said. Kevin was cracking up behind me. "No I just . . . I just heard about them . . . from a friend."

Maybe we weren't on such a roll. Walking back on Sunset Boulevard, we noticed that the only other people walking were bums and mentally retarded people. We caught a city bus, which was an even bigger freak show than the street. There was a man in the back with no pants on. And no underwear.

Through the first couple days of the trip, Kevin and I were pretty casual about things. When we were away from Billy and Nick we would goof around and act like tourists, making stupid jokes or staring at people or taking pictures of things like the movie theater that looked like a spaceship.

But the day before the showcase, that began to change. We started to feel the pressure. We walked down to Melrose that night and went to the Starbucks. We didn't meet any girls or talk to anyone. We barely talked ourselves. It was like we were athletes before the big game. We wanted to chill out and stay quiet and prepare ourselves mentally for what was coming.

The morning of the showcase, the four of us went out to breakfast. Nick had spoken to Chris Houghton and Martha from Silverlake. They were excited to see us play. Some of the other people from their management team were going to be there too. One of their assistants even called Nick to make sure we knew how to get to the club.

That afternoon we hung out at the Lab house and eventually started getting dressed. Nick had a new shirt he was going to wear. Kevin had some cool new jeans. Billy wanted me to wear sunglasses onstage, to make me look older, though previously everyone had liked the fact that I looked so young. This was different I guess.

At six we headed out. Our gig was right in the heart of the

famous Sunset Strip. Billy pointed out the famous clubs, the Whiskey, the Roxy, the Rainbow. We parked the van behind our club and loaded in. It was very chaotic. There was hardly any room to move anything and there were three bands and no one was cooperating. The spirit of competition was heavy in the air. I heard Billy start to argue with someone, and for the first time ever, Billy backed down.

One good thing: we had our own tiny dressing room. We hung out there, and eventually Chris and Martha appeared. They looked different now. They looked older and *harder* in some way. Chris was wearing a suit and a thick watch. His eyes were half-closed and slightly bloodshot. Still, he made sure to shake all of our hands and wish us luck. Martha said nothing, and they left.

We were going on second. Kevin and I snuck down the hall and watched the first band. They were much older than us, veterans of the local scene it looked like. Their singer was super flamboyant and was running around in a dress. People were laughing at his jokes between songs. But they joked around too much. Even though they were totally pro, no one took them seriously.

Then it was our turn. I had planned on wearing sunglasses, but the stage was so dark I didn't want to trip over something. Billy didn't notice anyway. Everyone was worried about themselves. We set up, plugged in, and Kevin counted us in.

The first song was a little rough. Eventually though, Billy and Nick rose to the occasion, as did Kevin and I. We got better with each song. By the end, we were dead-on. Kevin and I were even doing some of the extra stuff we did when we

217

were feeling confident. Still, there was a strange vacuum feeling on that stage. We felt farther apart than usual. We felt separated. I figured that was natural, like here we were, our dreams coming true, playing this huge showcase in LA. Each member of the band was experiencing it his own way. It made sense. It did to me anyway.

★ ★ ★ **77** ★ ★ ★

Then it was over and we were done and the next band's roadies yelled at us to get our stuff off. Some guy in a headset started screaming at us too. We packed up fast. I was sweating more from the backstage chaos than I had from the gig.

Finally we had everything in the van and we went to the dressing room and collapsed. And waited.

Chris and Martha did not come to our dressing room. Nick tried to find them in the club. He tried calling Chris on his cell phone. Chris finally called back. He would meet us in twenty minutes, out front.

We changed into clean shirts in the van and walked around to the front of the club. Nick and I leaned against a Mercedes parked at the curb. Exactly on time, Chris appeared. He smiled, shook hands, congratulated us on a great gig. He pulled Nick aside and said something to him. He and Nick went inside the club.

"Man," said Billy. We were dying of nerves. I lay back on the hood of the Mercedes. Kevin pulled me off it. "What if that's a rapper's car?" he said. "You wanna get us killed?"

I laughed at that. Kevin laughed too. Billy didn't. He went inside the club. When he was gone Kevin and I really started laughing.

"Oh my God, we're about to get signed!" said Kevin. We high-fived.

"Yeah, but we gotta be cool," I said, watching a bunch of metal-heads walk by. The sidewalk outside the club was a parade of every kind of musician, goth, metal-head, groupie, drug dealer. . . .

"Can you believe we're down here?" said Kevin. "Can you believe this is happening?"

I shook my head.

"Remember jazz band?" he asked me. "What would Mr. Moran say if he could see us now?"

I grinned and shook my head.

★ ★ ★ **78** ★ ★ ★

Nick and Billy came out of the club. Chris came with them. I watched Chris as the three of them came toward us. He never looked at me. He never looked at Kevin. He looked around us, through us, into the traffic behind us. His large head was tanned and his face glowed, almost like he had makeup on, like he was an actor, like all of this was a TV show.

He veered off from Nick and Billy and hurried—nearly ran—down the sidewalk. That was not what I expected.

Nick and Billy came forward. Kevin and I stood upright,

both of us searching their faces. Nick looked right at me, then away. Billy kept his distance.

"Guys," said Nick. "I'm just going to say this now. I'm not going to drag it out."

"What is it," said Kevin. "They don't want us?"

"They like what we're doing and they think we're great but they think we need to make changes."

"What kind of changes?" said Kevin.

"They think we have the germ of something. They think we have potential. . . ."

I didn't like the sound of that. I looked down at my feet, at the tennis shoes I was wearing. They looked naive and innocent against the filthy sidewalk of the Sunset Strip.

"They're basically offering Billy and me a development deal. They're going to form a band around us."

"What does that mean?" said Kevin.

"They want us to replace you guys. You're too young. They like you, but you're too young. They have pro guys they want us to use."

"And what did you say?" said Kevin.

"We . . . we think we should take it. We want to stay down here anyway. And you guys still have school and stuff. . . ." Nick looked at the ground. His voice was suddenly muffled and low.

"*School?*" said Kevin, loudly. "I don't have school. I just *graduated.*"

"Yeah, but you know—"

"And anyway, we're part of this," said Kevin, a sudden anger coming into his voice. "We're part of the sound. They can't find anyone who can do this better than we can."

"They want a slightly different sound anyway," said Nick. "More radio friendly. Less frantic."

"We're not *frantic*," said Kevin. He practically shouted it. On his face there was terrible pain. He looked at me for support. I didn't know what to say.

"And I'm eighteen," stammered Kevin. "Since when is that too young? They're obviously just trying to break us up. They obviously just want us out."

No one answered him.

"You're not going to let them do that are you?" said Kevin. He was losing it. His face was breaking down. He was going to start crying in a second. "You can't let them do that," Kevin continued. "Who are they, anyway? They're sleazy music industry people. They'll tell you anything. We're *a band*. We're Tiny Masters."

Nick said nothing. I watched him. I watched Billy. It was weird because for one brief moment, I saw it from Nick and Billy's side. Maybe we were too young. Maybe pro guys would make them better. But that wasn't true. Pro guys wouldn't care. Pro guys never cared. And anyway, great bands didn't sell out their original members. Great bands always had integrity about stuff like that. And it came through in the music. It was part of the soul of a band.

"How long have you known about this?" I heard myself ask Nick.

"They first said something a couple days ago," he answered. "We tried to convince them. . . ."

"But you couldn't," I said. "So you caved."

221

"What can we do?" said Nick. "They have the power."

"C'mon man, what would you do?" said Billy, from behind Nick.

I didn't answer. For the first time in a long time I felt superior to Nick and Billy. I was coming all the way around to my original opinion of them: they were amateurs.

Then I thought of my own situation. I was standing on the Sunset Strip; in Los Angeles, California; getting fired from the best band I'd ever seen by a guy in a suit.

I was seventeen.

Kevin knocked into someone walking by. He was falling apart. He was crying. He turned and started walking as fast as he could down the sidewalk. He looked like a crazy person.

"Kevin," I yelled after him.

"Hey Kev!" said Nick, calling after him.

Nobody moved to go after him. So I did. I tried walking, but he was going too fast. I started to jog, then to run, but he was running himself. . . .

★★★ **79** ★★★

It took several blocks to catch Kevin. I ran up beside him and grabbed his arm. He yanked free from me, ran faster, cocked his fist, and punched the side mirror of a parked car. The mirror shattered and broke off the side of the door. Kevin gasped with pain. He stumbled and gripped his fist. He fell between two parked cars. His fist was bleeding. He was sobbing. I bent down to him.

"I got nothing," he whimpered, his head resting on the dirty pavement. "I gave up everything for this and now I have nothing!"

"You didn't give up everything," I said. I tried to look at his fist. His whole hand was bleeding.

"You don't understand. I wanted this more than anything."

"I understand, trust me," I said. I tried lifting him by the shirt. "You can't lie in the street," I told him. "You gotta get up."

"How can they do this to us?" he muttered. "How?"

I pulled him to his feet and wiped off his shirt. I checked to make sure the owner of the car wasn't around. There was a side street going up the hill. I led him up it. We sat on the sidewalk, against a building.

Neither of us spoke. I looked at his hand. A sliver of glass was sticking out of his knuckle. I pulled it out.

"Ow!" he said, pulling his hand away. He yanked a bandanna from his pocket and wrapped it around his fist. He wiped his tears with his good hand. "Now what do we do?" he said.

"I don't know," I said. Below us I watched Sunset Boulevard.

"How do we get back to Portland?" asked Kevin.

"They're not leaving us. They'll take us back."

"They said they're staying. Didn't you hear them?"

"So we'll take a bus or something."

Kevin lowered his head between his knees. "I think I'm going to kill myself," he said.

"You're not going to kill yourself," I said, throwing a bit of gravel into the street.

He lowered his head between his knees. I looked down at the Strip. I assumed Nick and Billy would come find us, but when a half hour passed and there was no sign of them I began to wonder.

"You got a quarter?" I said.

Kevin dug in his pocket and gave me one.

I went back down to the Strip. I started walking. That street, I swear, it was nonstop action: clubs and bars, bands and groupies. I watched everything. I wanted to hate it but I couldn't. I loved this world. I loved being a musician. What had happened tonight wasn't going to change that.

I walked until I found a pay phone. I dialed the familiar number of my house in Portland.

The phone picked up. "Hello?"

"Hey, Dad," I said.

"Peter!" he said. I'd never heard my father so happy. "What's happening? How's it going?"

"Not that good at the moment . . ." I said, staring through the smudged glass of the phone booth.

"What's up? Did you play the showcase?"

"Yeah we played it."

"And?"

I tried to talk but I couldn't. I closed my eyes for a moment. "Listen, Dad, we're kind of in a jam. . . ."

"Pete," said my dad. "Are you all right?"

"Yeah, I'm fine. It's just . . . things are kinda . . . falling apart."

"Where are you? What street?"

"I'm on Sunset."

"Sunset and what?"

I didn't know. I had to ask someone. "Just stay there," said my dad. "I'll call someone."

"But Dad?" I said.

"Yeah?"

"I still want to do this. No matter what."

"I know."

★ ★ ★ 80 ★ ★ ★

Thirty minutes after I hung up the phone an old friend of my dad's, Ms. Jacqueline Delacroix, pulled up in a red BMW convertible. Kevin and I reluctantly crawled in. Ms. Delacroix smoked cigarettes as she drove us up the winding roads of the Hollywood Hills. She was not concerned we had just been kicked out of a band. She had been kicked out of many bands. She produced the music on commercials now, and had a real estate business. Her house, she announced as we pulled into her driveway, was worth $2.5 million.

I never got the exact story of what the connection with my dad was. I suspect she was an ex-girlfriend from way back. She asked me a few questions about him, but not too much. Inside her house we met Sierra, her thirteen-year-old daughter. Sierra was not impressed with us. She knew lots of musicians. Frances Bean Cobain went to her school.

The next morning someone from Delacroix Real Estate made arrangements for our drums and stuff to be picked up and shipped back home. I made a feeble offer to pay for this, but Jacqueline laughed and waved her cigarette at me.

We sat around the pool all that afternoon. It was very weird, trying to feel bad, while the housekeeper brought us homemade mango smoothies. That night we played video games with Sierra. The next morning the housekeeper drove us to the airport and we flew home.

★★★ 81 ★★★

Three weeks later, I was sitting among the familiar sounds of the Woodridge Lanes bowling alley: rolling balls, crashing pins, the bad Top 40 on the sound system. I sipped my Coke and watched Robert Hatch lift his orange bowling ball out of the return rack. It was my second Coke of the night, and I was drinking it too fast. I put it down. My foot tapped nervously against the floor.

"Don't worry, she'll be here," said Lauren. "She had to babysit until nine."

"Jeez," said Robert. "You'd think a senior would be done with babysitting."

"She happens to like it," said Lauren.

I watched Robert. He faced the pins and lined himself up. He walked forward, held the ball out, swung it back, launched it down the lane. The orange swirl pattern spun slightly as it rolled. It hit with surprising power, knocking down eight pins. Robert was getting better at bowling.

Lauren took her turn. I took mine. I sat back down on the plastic bench and drank my Coke.

Then that voice. "Hi you guys," it said behind me. It was Margaret. "Sorry I'm late."

Lauren hurried to greet her. Robert waved hi. I stood up awkwardly.

Lauren led Margaret to the bench. Everyone became very nervous. No one seemed able to speak. Lauren left Margaret and joined Robert at the scorer's table. It was a not very subtle attempt to leave us alone.

"Hey," I said to Margaret. "What's up?"

"Nothing."

"Wanna sit down?" I moved our coats to make room.

She sat. She couldn't look at me right away. When she did, she smiled. I felt myself relax. It was great to see her and to be close to her. I had seen her at school but we hadn't talked.

"I heard about the band," she said. "Sorry."

I shrugged. "It's a tough business."

"Jennifer told me about Kevin, and his hand, and how you pulled him out of the street. The whole thing sounds . . . incredible."

"I was glad he freaked out," I said. "If he hadn't, I would have."

She smiled at that. "So now what are you gonna do?"

I smiled. "Nothing. Maybe do jazz band. Actually, I think I might . . . start my own band."

"Really?" she said.

I nodded. I sipped my Coke. We didn't talk for a while.

"Robert said you and Brian broke up," I said.

"Yeah. We never really got on track, I guess."

"That's too bad."

"Yeah."

"Hey, Margaret!" interrupted Lauren. "Are you playing the next game? Did you get bowling shoes?"

227

"Right here," said Margaret, holding them up. She kicked off her normal shoes and began to put them on.

"Hey, thanks for coming tonight," I said.

"I wanted to see you," said Margaret, still bent over. "I never get to talk to you at school."

"I know," I said. "I was hoping we could hang out a little."

She looked up from tying her shoe. Her expression tried to say, *I'm not ready for that, not yet.* But I knew her so well. I knew her like I knew myself. She wanted to. She couldn't hide it.

She tightened her shoe strings. She stood, smoothed her skirt, and went to find a bowling ball.

Later, in the parking lot, there was a lot of awkward talk about who was riding home with whom. Finally the girls decided that Lauren and Margaret were going in Lauren's car. Robert would drop me off.

Of course Lauren and Robert had to make out for several minutes before they could leave.

I stood with Margaret under the parking lot lights. We both leaned against the side of Lauren's car. I wanted to say something. I felt words come to my mouth, but I couldn't speak them. So I took her hand.

She didn't mind. She let me. We both looked at the ground. We held hands and didn't speak. Eventually she held my hand with both of hers. Our shoulders touched. When I turned toward her, she stared into my eyes. I stared into hers.

Then she let go and got in Lauren's car without saying a word.

+++

Robert was still with Lauren. I walked away from the car, kicking at the gravel in the parking lot. I gazed at the rows of empty cars, the black sky. I really did want to start my own band. I hadn't done anything yet, but now that I had told Margaret, it suddenly seemed more real. It would be hard. It would be a lot of work. But I could do it. I knew *how* to do it.

Robert and Lauren finally separated. Robert led me to his car. As he pulled out, we passed Lauren's car. I looked for Margaret through her fogged window. I saw her black coat, her shoulder, then her face as we passed. I waved to her. She waved back.

Then I sat back and thought how much there was to do, and how much was yet to come.